I0552856

A Novel

J.D. Wade & Chase Connor

Chase Connor Books
The Lion Fish Press
www.chaseconnor.com
www.thelionfishpress.com

To the extent that the image or images on the cover of this book depict a person or persons, such person or persons are merely models, and are not intended to portray any character or characters feature in the book.

Cover models are not intended to illustrate specific people and the content does not refer to models' actual acts, identity, history, beliefs or behavior. No characters depicted in this ebook are intended to represent real people. Models are used for illustrative purposes only.

Book Cover Designed By: Allen T. St. Clair, ©2020 J.D. Wade & Chase Connor

Published By:

The Lion Fish Press
539 W. Commerce St #227
Dallas, TX 75208

© Copyright 2020 J.D. Wade & Chase Connor

All rights reserved. Without limiting the rights under copyright reserved above, no part of this publication may be reproduced, stored in or introduced into a retrieval system, or transmitted, in any form, or by any means (electronic, mechanical, photocopying, recording or otherwise), without the prior written permission of the copyright owner.

AUTHORS' NOTE:
This is a work of fiction. Names, characters, places, and incidents either are the product of the authors' imagination or are used fictitiously, and any resemblance to actual persons, living or dead, business establishments, events, or locales is entirely coincidental. None of this is real.

Ebook ISBN 978-1-951860-14-1
Paperback ISBN 978-1-951860-17-2

Also by J.D. Wade

The Advisor

First Comes Love (forthcoming)

Also by Chase Connor

LGBTQ+ YA Books

Just a Dumb Surfer Dude: A Gay Coming-of-Age Tale
Just a Dumb Surfer Dude 2: For the Love of Logan
Just a Dumb Surfer Dude 3: Summer Hearts
Gavin's Big Gay Checklist
A Surplus of Light (**Also in Spanish** – *Un Excedente de Luz*)
The Guy Gets Teddy
GINJUH

LGBTQ+ New Adult and Lit Fic

A Tremendous Amount of Normal
The Gravity of Nothing
Between Enzo & the Universe (**Also in Spanish** – *Entrez Enzo y el Universo*)

LGBTQ+ YA & MG Fantasy

A Million Little Souls

A Point Worth LGBTQ Paranormal Romances

Jacob Michaels Is Tired (Book 1)
Jacob Michaels Is Not Crazy (Book 2)
Jacob Michaels Is Not Jacob Michaels (Book 3)
Jacob Michaels Is Not Here (Book 4)
Jacob Michaels Is Trouble (Book 5)
CARNAVAL (A Point Worth LGBTQ Paranormal Romance Story)
Jacob Michaels Is Dead (Book 6)

Erotica

Bully

Audiobooks

A Surplus of Light: A Gay Coming-of-Age Tale (Narrated by Brian Lore Evans)
Between Enzo & the Universe (Narrated by Brian Lore Evans)

J.D. & Chase would like to thank their beta-readers, The Lion Fish Press, and Words with Friends for bringing them joy during bouts of procrastination.

A Note from the Authors:

This story was started before we, and the world, became aware of COVD-19. For the sake of the story, and enjoyment of our readers, we have chosen to pretend COVID-19 doesn't exist (wouldn't that be great?). Obviously, there isn't enough social distancing, masks, and hand washing to throw a party with over a hundred attendees.

Be responsible in reality, but enjoy the story.

Stay safe.

Stay healthy.

Chapters

Chapter 1
L.S.P.

Uncle Harry's and Uncle Vic's party wasn't even close to beginning when I had finished dressing and was standing in front of the Victorian Cheval mirror in the corner of my room. It was an antique—the mirror that is—that I had been denied permission to move out of my room. Uncle Harry had gotten up in years and didn't feel he was steady enough on his feet to carry it himself, and due to my perceived accident-prone nature, he forbade me from moving it. He'd only ever seen me break a vase one time when I was a rambunctious six-year-old visiting over the summer with my parents. Uncle Harry didn't know how to let things go. The mirror was solid mahogany and real glass, carved cabriole legs—an antique he'd purchased on one of his trips to London in the 80s—it was broader and taller than me and weighed nearly as much. With Uncle Harry's Parkinson's and selective memory about my coordination, the idea of moving the mirror presented a problem when I had first moved in with him and Uncle Vic.

Uncle Vic felt as though he was sturdy and reliable enough to move the mirror, but Uncle Harry had nixed the idea. *Hernia surgery at your age?* Uncle Harry had scoffed. *You'd die on the table. Of course, I could use the Vicodin if you somehow managed to survive...* Uncle Vic and I had tried to convince Uncle Harry that maybe Vic wouldn't get a hernia if the two of us worked together, and Harry wouldn't have to worry about me dropping it. That was quickly dismissed as a possibility as well. Of course, I had offered to hire movers—who were less likely to drop things—to come over and move the mirror for us. That was deemed unacceptable due to my uncle's persnickety nature. We went back and forth for days before I realized that Uncle Harry simply liked the mirror where it was and had no intention of ever letting it be moved to another room.

After living with my uncles for a week, I was beginning to love the mirror, so I was slowly deciding it was not a hill I wanted to die upon. There were more important things in life to worry about. Besides, after a shower, it was nice to be able to escape the steamy, claustrophobic, closet-sized bathroom just off my bedroom and still be able to groom myself without merely guessing at what I was doing with my hair. Uncle Vic seemed uninterested in the fact that the mirror situation had been resolved quietly, and Uncle Harry was glad that I was no longer obsessed with getting it out of my room. We all won in the end. Of course, the desire to move the mirror—and not break it—overcame me at least five times a day. Just to prove something to myself and Uncle Harry. But I never did.

I wonder if he... The thought came from out of nowhere as I stood in front of the mirror, looking at myself, but I quickly shook it off.

Those thoughts were not welcome on the day of the party.

Sounds of the last-minute details of the party being taken care of carried down the hallway to my room, muffled only by my closed bedroom door. Though I couldn't hear exactly what they were saying, I knew Uncle Harry and Uncle Vic were arguing. I didn't really need to hear what they were saying, and I didn't have to decipher the tone of the sounds coming down the hall. The two of them always argued. It was their favorite hobby and one they could continue with regardless of what age did to their physical abilities. Disagreeing about the tiniest things is a sport that even the oldest people in the world can participate in as long as they retain the ability to speak and keep at least a spark of spite.

I'm not saying that Uncle Vic and Uncle Harry fought because they had grown to hate each other after nearly fifty years of togetherness or anything like that. Some older people do crossword puzzles or watch *Jeopardy!* to keep their mental faculties sharp. My uncles just preferred snark and witty comebacks to trivia when it came to mental exercise. It was a game to them, the arguing. One of them would express an opinion about the way something should be done, and the other took the opposition, even if they didn't think it was correct. Even if they didn't couldn't care less about how things were being done. In the end, it didn't even matter who ended up being right. The winner was determined by who was feisty enough to see the fight through to the bitter end without giving up, or which one of them came up with the most devastating insult. Ultimately, they'd laugh, kiss (*disgusting*), and carry on with their day.

Until the next opportunity to fight presented itself. Most likely over how to load the dishwasher or organize the fridge door.

Condiments go in the door; milk goes on the top shelf!

As I stood there and looked in the mirror, I couldn't help but wonder what I was getting myself into with the party. Being surrounded by hundreds of my uncles' friends all evening, making small talk with people I didn't know, trying to be as witty as my uncles—it sounded like a nightmare. *Actually, it just doesn't sound like me.* I can't carry a drink around making polite, interesting conversation without looking like anything but a party crasher, so being witty is way out of my skill set.

In the mirror, I saw myself for what I was—an introverted hot mess with no fashion sense and a rapidly developing ulcer due to the cyclic thoughts about all of the people coming to the party. I did my best to make myself look presentable in front of the mirror, straightening my collar, running my fingers through my hair to make it do what it was supposed to, and making sure all of my buttons aligned. Uncle Harry's voice was traveling down the hall outside of my room, working its way to the front door as I shifted my glasses on my face, hoping they were straight so that I didn't look insane to the guests.

"*I told that bitch five o'clock, Victor!*" Uncle Harry was hissing as he looked down the hallway towards the kitchen when he opened my door. "*I'm old, but I can still read a clock!*"

Uncle Harry's angry expression melted away instantly, as though he had never been mad, and a smile alighted on his face when he turned to look at me.

"Getting ready for the party, darling?" He cooed, his head wobbling slightly on his shoulders, thanks to his Parkinson's. "We're just having a bit of trouble with the caterer."

"Ah," I said. "I was wondering which bitch you were referencing."

"There are so many." He sighed, his hand relaxing on the doorknob. "So? Party?"

"As ready as I'll ever be." I shrugged as I turned to present myself.

Uncle Harry's face dropped, and his hand fell from the doorknob.

"You're not wearing that?" He brought a hand to his mouth dramatically.

"What's wrong with what I'm wearing?" I asked.

I turned back to the mirror to inspect my jeans and long-sleeve button-down. What had I done to make Uncle Harry react in horror? Had I spilled something on myself? Did he think blue-on-blue was a wrong choice? Was it that I had rolled up my sleeves? My kicks were brand new, so he couldn't possibly have found offense with them.

"Russ," Uncle Harry asked from behind me, "why would you do this to yourself?"

"Do what?" I threw my hands up. "What's wrong?"

"There will be no fewer than a dozen vicious old queens at this party." He retorted. "It's as if you *want* to be read to filth."

"I know what vicious old queens do, Harry." I laughed. "I live with two of them. They usually just pick on each other and talk about everyone else behind their backs. I'm good."

"Well," He waved a dismissive hand before setting it back on the doorknob, "your Uncle Vic and I love you, so we save our bile for each other. Tonight will be different. Many of the people you'll be around tonight don't know you well enough to love you. Aside from vicious old queens, there will be some young men you might want to actually show interest. Maybe a different shirt—"

"Harry." I stopped him. "This shirt is fine."

"What of the lesbians?" Harry clutched his other hand to his chest. "They may mistake you for one of their own. Denim on denim? Darling, you're either a lesbian or Jo from *The Facts of Life*. Which is basically the same thing, I suppose, but—"

"Jo? *The Facts of Life*?" I frowned.

"Having a young person in the house is so rewarding." Uncle Harry deadpanned. "Now I hope the lesbians do try to adopt you as one of their own."

Harry's hand dropped from the doorknob as he clutched his chest and twirled around to leave my bedroom.

"*Vic!*" Uncle Harry screeched down the hallway. "*We have a lesbian infestation! Pour me a finger—two fingers—of bourbon!*"

Then he was gone. I turned back to the mirror.

"*I do look like a lesbian,*" I mumbled to myself.

Uncle Harry's dramatics were uncalled for, though. Obviously, it takes more than one lesbian to constitute an infestation. There was no point in trying to fix my outfit or try something else on for the party. My laundry hamper was full, and all of my clothes that were clean were either too casual or too formal for the party. Either way, the "vicious old queens" would have their say in the end. Accepting that what I had on was what I'd be wearing for the rest of the night was my best course of action. I could always hope that my outfit was so offensive that everyone would avoid me, and the chore of pretending to be interesting and making small talk would resolve itself.

The house was nearly silent as I exited my bedroom and made my way towards the kitchen. Uncle Vic's muffled voice reached my ears, though I could tell he was on the phone and no longer arguing with Uncle Harry. He was probably on the phone, sorting out the catastrophic problem with the caterers. When I entered the big transitional style kitchen, Uncle Harry was sitting on one of the stools in front of the big island, sipping a dark amber liquid from a highball glass. Uncle Vic spoke calmly and evenly into his cell phone, though he paused to give me a smile and a wave before returning to his task.

Harry looked positively unsettled from our interaction in the bedroom, which only made my eyes roll back in my head as I shuffled over and lifted myself up onto one of the empty stools on the other side of the island.

"*Drama queen,*" I mumbled.

"I'm sorry, darling." Uncle Harry quipped, the highball glass halfway to his mouth. "Lower your voice. Everything is positively deafening over that whisper of an outfit."

Uncle Vic slapped at Uncle Harry's shoulder reproachfully as he listened to the person on the other end of the phone.

"I get it," I grumbled. "My clothes are boring and plain. I'm a bad gay man. Shoot me."

"I would need to lay down drop cloths first, but you seem to be wearing them." Harry sniped before taking another sip from his drink.

"Sooooo bitchy," I said.

"My dear nephew," Harry lowered his glass as Vic finished up his phone call, "I don't point out the glaringly—and offensively—obvious fashion faux pas I see to *not* be called a bitch."

My eyes were rolling once again.

"Thank you, that would be lovely," Vic said into the phone. "Goodbye."

Vic tapped the phone screen with his thumb and laid it down on the island before turning his attention to me.

"You look handsome as always, Russ." He smiled. "Don't let this old fart tell you otherwise."

"Old fart?" Harry nearly choked on his drink. "I'm simply trying to get the boy to understand LSP, Victor. Is that so wrong of me?"

"L...SP?" I asked.

"*Lesbian Safety Precautions.*" Uncle Vic waved me off as he turned to Uncle Harry. "Stop it. Drink your bourbon and relax. The caterers will be here in thirty minutes. Things will be fine."

"It will be nearly six o'clock then, Victor!" Harry was scandalized. "The party starts at seven!"

"Professionals can set up in minutes, Harry." Victor reached over to pat his hand. "Stop worrying so much."

"Fine, fine." Harry lifted his drink again, his head still wobbling slightly. "But you know Dan and Rafi will show up early enough to qualify as hosts."

"Just as I know Bang Bang will be hours late." Uncle Vic agreed. "That reporter from *The Gazette* will be here at six-thirty to talk about the party and the *end of an era*."

"What's *Lesbian Safety Precautions*?" I asked.

Uncle Vic rolled his eyes as Harry sipped his bourbon.

"Your Uncle here," He jabbed a thumb in Harry's general direction, "has a theory that the lesbians will absorb any wayfaring young gay into their inner circle and get them to do their bidding. He has a severe dislike of—"

"*Distrust!*" Harry corrected him.

"—distrust of lesbians." Vic shrugged. "Though we count many as friends, as you know. It's probably old age and senility, honestly, and—"

"The year before I met your Uncle Victor," Harry interjected, "I was spending a summer—"

"Lord, help us." Vic sighed.

"—in New York. I was very shy then—"

"If you can believe that," Vic added.

"—and totally hopeless when it came to approaching other guys at the bars. So—"

"Now he just drags them around the dumpster behind Taco Bell." Vic winked at me.

"—I struck up a conversation with a *seemingly* harmless lesbian—cute as a button, no taller than my shoulder, honestly—"

"Which used to be higher."

"—*if you don't shut the hell up, Victor!*" Harry snapped. Uncle Vic smiled at me, then turned to busy himself at the sink. "Well, we got to talking, one thing led to another, and I found myself in upstate New York helping a legion of lesbians raise a barn for some commune they planned to start. *Upstate New York, Russ!* To think of it now—"

"I'm surprised you can remember it," Vic mumbled.

Luckily, Uncle Harry didn't quite catch what Uncle Vic had said.

"—makes me shudder. If it hadn't been for their exceptional abilities in procuring weed and finding the best artisanal cheese shops, it would have been a total loss. Either way, I still returned home after summer with a bowl cut, two pairs of Dr. Martens from a thrift store, and still a virgin!"

"Imagine," Vic mumbled again. "*That* was once *pure.*"

"I didn't see a single cock the entire summer!" Harry stated with finality before raising his glass once more.

"Don't say 'cock,' Harry." I grimaced.

He gave a dismissive wave before slamming the rest of his bourbon.

"Look, I'll change if it's that big of a deal." I shrugged.

"Don't you dare, Russ," Uncle Vic said, shooting a look at Uncle Harry. "Tonight is a celebration of being exactly who we are for the last forty years. You look very handsome."

"You look like you want to raise a barn and ruin my summer. Which could be my last." Harry corrected him. "But I suppose Victor is right. This party is about all of us and not just your dreadful shirt. Maybe a nice kerchief or—"

"I'm not wearing a kerchief."

Harry started to open his mouth again.

"Or a pocket square, ascot or cravat." I stopped him. "I'll look like a rainbow if you had your way with my outfit."

Okay, so that wasn't totally fair. Both of my uncles looked completely party-ready without looking as though they were about to take the stage on a cruise ship. Uncle Harry, still wiry, but a bit shorter with age, had on black slacks, an emerald green button-down, and a nice light blazer over it. Uncle Vic, tall and broad, was adorned similarly, but red was his chosen shirt color. They looked like Christmas without the overdone parade. Without asking, I knew that they had coordinated with the other older gay men who were coming to the party so that they all wore a shirt with a color of the rainbow. I could imagine the Instagram pictures that would appear in the morning.

"Let me just go see what I have that will suit you." Harry was off his stool and out of the kitchen before I could object.

Uncle Vic and I were left in the kitchen, smiling at each other from across the island.

"He moves quickly for men and fashion." Uncle Vic winked. "But ask him to take out the trash, and…well, it's been fifty years. Too late to smother him in his sleep."

"Is it, though?" I snorted.

Uncle Vic leaned across the island to pat my hand.

"If he comes in here with a rainbow kerchief, just wear it, Russ." He said. "Harry is so proud that we've reached this night."

I twisted my jaw back and forth, mulling this over.

"Fine." I sighed. "I can be his paper doll for one night."

"That's my boy." Vic patted my hand once more before standing up straight again.

"Vic," I asked, "what's he going to do without the bar? I mean, retirement? I can't imagine Harry not keeping busy all day."

Uncle Victor chuckled to himself as he leaned back against the counter behind him.

"You as well," I added. "*A Straight Line* was everything to you guys. To all the queer people in the area. What now?"

"Well," Vic mulled this over, "the bar will still be there for all of the queer people around here. They'll still have a home. And you're here now. I guess we have a free house sitter for all of those trips we always said we'd take. Free house sitter? Free time? Maybe I'll get Harry to France for a second time after all?"

"Really?"

"We'll probably buy some recliners and watch *Murder, She Wrote*," Vic admitted. "We have the whole box set on DVD."

"I have no idea what that is, but I'm sure it's something fascinating for—"

Uncle Vic gave me a stern look.

"For people of a certain age." I smiled impishly.

"*People of a certain age?*" Vic glowered. "We can send you back to your parents, Russ."

"I'm twenty-five years old." I laughed. "You can't send me back to my parents. You can't send me anywhere."

"We can make you sleep in the yard." He quipped mirthfully.

"Fine." I relented. "But you guys are *people of a certain age*. No offense intended."

"I hope Harry returns with a rainbow ascot and leather chaps." He replied.

I laughed loudly.

"*Don't forget to take your pills while you're in there, Harry!*" Uncle Vic turned his attention from me to scream towards the hallway. "*If you don't take your evening meds now, you're going to forget once the party starts!*"

Uncle Harry screamed back something that indicated he had heard. I smiled at Vic as he settled back into leaning against the kitchen counter. After nearly fifty years of togetherness, my two uncles still looked after each other. Vic gave me a smile.

"When you find the love of your life, Russ, make sure you take care of them." He advised. "Someone has to remind the idiots to look after their health, after all."

I shifted on the stool.

"Love." I scoffed.

"Love," Vic repeated. "You know? The thing that makes the world go 'round?"

"Right. Fuck science. Let's give philosophy the credit."

"To be so young and jaded." Vic pretended to swoon. "It's a wonder the boys aren't absolutely busting down your door."

"Ow." I laughed, though it wasn't genuine.

"Listen," Vic was moving to lean across the counter once again, "tonight is special. It means a lot to your Uncle Harry. And to me. Try not to be too much of a cynic."

"Okay." I agreed. "I mean, I'll try."

"Russ," He smiled as he reached over to pat my hand, "whenever the gays gather—particularly for a special occasion—it's simply magical. You won't have to try."

Uncle Vic was waxing poetic, but I didn't want to ruin the poignancy of it by making some offhanded quip, so I chose to remain silent.

"Now," he announced, "I need to go check myself over. What if the reporter from *The Gazette* wants photos?"

"All right."

"Hey," He stopped next to me and bopped me lightly under my chin with the fleshy part of his fist, "how are you doing? Really?"

I waved him off. "I'm fine."

Uncle Vic's eyes bore into mine.

"I swear." I gave him my best chuckle. "Things will be fine once I really settle in."

"Okay." He gave my chin another light tap before resuming forward momentum. "I have to pretty myself up for those pictures!"

Uncle Vic received a mere smile from me as he peacocked away, off to primp while we waited on the doorbell to signal the arrival of the caterer the and reporter from *The Gazette*. I stayed perched upon the stool in the kitchen, mulling over my thoughts. The kitchen I was sitting in had once been all Formica and linoleum; at one time, white appliances and fluorescent lights had done their best to brighten up a room with no windows. Now, the kitchen had large windows that looked out over the property at the back of the house where gorgeous Silver Maples and Red Oaks dotted the acreage. The floor of the kitchen was now hardwood, and the countertops were quartz. Solid wood cabinets, painted black, didn't darken the kitchen, thanks to the numerous windows. Pendant lights now hung over the island and kitchen table. The room no longer looked like the sad, worn down, outdated kitchen it had been when Vic and Harry bought the place.

The first time my parents had brought me to visit my uncles, the house had been in shambles as repairs and renovations were ongoing. All my uncles' money had been sunk into their business venture—*A Straight Line*—and it was just starting to turn a real profit for them. This was twenty years into owning the bar, mind you. With their first real profits saved up, they had bought a house that sat on plenty of land and needed a lot of love, excited to bring more joy to their lives. As the years went by and the bar expanded, so did my uncles' income. What was once virtually a hovel was now a home that a person would see on an interior design website. Or, at least, Pinterest.

I didn't know it at the time, but Mom and Dad had initially scoffed at Uncle Harry's and Uncle Vic's idea to open a gay bar in their tiny rural town. Not only was it likely to go under, dragging them with it, they also worried about how my uncles would be treated in the community. Their safety was always a concern. Of course, it hadn't been easy, keeping *A Straight Line* afloat—or even open—at times, but Vic and Harry had persevered. Forty years after the doors had opened at *A Straight Line*, they had made enough money and felt it was time to enjoy their twilight years. The bar was put up for sale, as is—which was in pretty good condition with a giant built-in clientele—and Harry and Vic took their leave. *A Straight Line* would no longer be theirs in a matter of days.

However, like any real gay men, they had to have the final say. One last party to commemorate the previous forty years of hard work, headache, heartache, happiness, sorrow, friendship, loss, and joy. *A Straight Line* had meant so much to them from the very beginning. Now it was so much more than a dream of two gay men desperately in love, looking to change the world. It had become a sanctuary for all the LGBTQ-plus people within a hundred miles of Littleburg, Iowa—*The Biggest Little City on the Wapsipinicon River. A Straight Line*—and my uncles—had been there for the LGBTQ-plus community when no one else was.

Though I was definitely a cynic—especially when it came to love—I knew my uncles, their bar, and this final party to celebrate it all was important. So, I affixed a smile to my face, gave myself a mental pep talk, and decided that for at least one night, I would believe in the magic of being part of the LGBTQ-plus community. Even if sitting in front of the T.V. in my pajamas sounded way more appealing than trying to be interested in small talk with people I hadn't seen in years or never even met before.

Chapter 2
Caterers & Columnists A Comin'

Although strings of lights, some that were plain white and others that were every color of the rainbow, had been hung in advance of the party, there was still a lot for the caterers and party planner to do. From the kitchen windows, I could see that the lights were hung tautly from tree to tree in the enormous backyard. The gazebo, about ten yards from the giant Bluestone patio, white and gleaming in the summer sun, had rainbow bunting and lights adorning it as well. Tiki torches lined the stone walkway that led from the patio to the gazebo and were just waiting to be lit. A large square in the yard had been roped off—a temporary dance floor—with a DJ booth to one side. Clusters of vinyl balloons—in all the colors of the rainbow, of course—stuck up from the yard, suspended in the air on thin iron stakes. Uncle Harry had struck a deal with Lamont's Auto Yard to borrow the balloons for the evening, and they had arrived and been staked in the yard by Lamont himself. All before I had risen from bed at mid-morning.

The house itself was mostly unadorned since most of the festivities would happen outside, but plenty of ambient lighting had been organized throughout the living room and kitchen. A few rainbow banners were hung here and there. Being summer, some people might need to step inside to cool off for a few moments, or to use the restroom, not to mention get more food, so the house couldn't go completely untouched by the festive décor. In the hour leading up to the arrival of the caterers, Uncle Harry and Uncle Vic mostly busied themselves rushing from room to room, making sure that everything would look presentable to their guests.

Close your bedroom door for fuck's sake, Russ! Uncle Harry had hissed at one point. *I don't want people thinking we live like animals. Or, God forbid, straight people.*

So, I had closed the door to the bedroom I was using. Once the last person excused themselves from the party, I would reopen the door and live like an animal once again. It wasn't really my fault that the bedroom I had taken over when I moved in with my uncles looked so...*plain.* I had arrived with very little to my name—mostly the clothes on my back and those I could fit into two suitcases, as well as my laptop. But I hadn't arrived with anything to make the room my own and hadn't had time to go out and shop for décor. It would have been pointless, anyway. Living with Uncle Harry and Vic was only supposed to be temporary, after all. The only thing in my room that Uncle Harry approved of was his antique mirror.

Why he didn't want to move the mirror was suddenly dawning on me.

As my uncles entertained themselves by looking busy, I found myself pacing the house, shuffling from room to room, as though I had never seen it before. Having lived with them for a week, there hadn't been much in the house my eyes hadn't taken in already, but taking a walk through their memories always made me smile a little. That was what their home was like—a shrine to their memories as a couple. Still chic and decorated expertly—as only a gay man can do—the house always managed to exude a lived-in, homey feel. Various sized frames decorated the mantelpiece, each holding pictures from their first trip to London. An old pouf they had purchased in Spain sat in front of the reading chair by the bay window in the den. A giant jar of seashells, stones, and sea glass they had collected along the Oregon and Washington coasts.

The wide hallway that ran from the entryway to the very back of the house—where the kitchen was located—was lined with black and white and color photographs framed and hung expertly. *The time they met Elizabeth Taylor, in L.A. with the Hollywood sign in the distance, on a boat with the Sydney Opera House behind them, hiking to Machu Pichu, memorable moments at* A Straight Line, *family members and friends, and a picture of the two of them for all forty-eight of their anniversaries.* It was an imposing hallway, so the framed photos adorning the walls on either side didn't make it look too cluttered.

I found myself standing in the hallway, just before six o'clock, my eyes flitting from one picture to another until they finally settled upon one. My uncles, together for almost seven years at that point—long before I was born—were standing in front of the old building that had once housed a restaurant. A year after the picture was taken, *A Straight Line* would be open. The smiles on their faces and their arms over each other's shoulders as they stood in front of the old restaurant made me smile. Another man stood behind them in the picture, his head several inches higher than theirs.

"That's Bang Bang." Uncle Vic's voice sounded from over my shoulder.

I stared at the handsome young face of the man in the photograph. Chiseled and traditionally masculine, pearly white teeth shone out from between curved lips.

"*That's* Bang Bang?" I repeated in awe. "It looks nothing like her."

"Well, she learned to contour before you came along." Uncle Vic chuckled as he looked over my shoulder at the photograph. "She was the first real friend we made in Littleburg. Buying the bar was Bang Bang's idea, of course."

"Of course." I chuckled.

"She knew if we could provide a stage, she could put butts in seats." Vic sighed. "She was right. After a few years."

I laughed.

"It took her a while to really find her groove and get people showing up regularly," Vic explained. "Now, they come from all over on Friday and Saturday nights to see Bang Bang sing and tell her dick jokes."

"No one tells a dick joke like a—"

"—queen trying to hide one." Uncle Vic finished the quote with me.

We both laughed at the memory as we stared at the picture.

"I've never seen her out of drag," I said simply.

"Well," Uncle Vic reached over my shoulder and ran his fingers along the bottom of the frame lovingly, "Bang Bang's so busy, now Morty is the persona she slips into from time to time to feel like her true self."

"*Morty?*" I snorted.

"Shhh." Uncle Vic teased. "Bang Bang would throw a shoe if she heard."

"Your secret's safe with me."

Uncle Vic grew quiet as I stared at the picture, amazed at seeing Northeastern Iowa's most famous drag queen out of drag for the first time ever. It was like seeing your teacher at the strip club, or your parole officer at the liquor store. Something just didn't seem right about seeing Bang Bang as Morty without her permission. It filled me with a vague sense of foreboding. Of course, she had been to Vic's and Harry's house often enough that, surely, she was aware of the picture in the hallway. If she had requested it, they would have taken it down in a hot second to appease her. Since it hung in the hallway, I had to assume that I wasn't intruding.

"Here's Morty again." Vic stepped away from me to point at another picture a few feet to my left.

I stepped over to look at the picture Vic's finger had pressed against. My uncles were seated at a table with a checkered cloth, the crystal blue sea behind them as the sun set on the horizon. To the other side of the table sat Bang Bang—*well, Morty, I guess*—and another man I didn't recognize. The man next to Bang Bang looked older than everyone else at the table—by at least a decade. He was thin with age, a bit sunken looking, though he smiled. They all held champagne flutes and looked positively jubilant. Probably drunk actually, but *jubilant* sounded better in my mind.

"When we all went to Santorini twenty-five years ago. We didn't really have the money for the trip, but Bang Bang is so persuasive." Vic explained wistfully. "That was our first night there. We all stayed shit-canned from sun up to sundown. The shirtless men, the seafood, the dancing, the sea…*the ouzo*. I'm surprised we all made it home, honestly. It was one of the best weeks of our lives."

I turned to stare at my uncle, finding his eyes on the photo and a sentimental curve to his lips. If I wasn't mistaken, his eyes looked watery.

"My God, Russ," He said, collecting himself, "we danced. Morty—or Bang Bang in most cases—could light up a place. Even if everyone in the room was ready to fight, he'd get them all on the dance floor. It was like we didn't go to Greece, but Greece came to us. You'd see it in Morty's eyes when Bang Bang would take over—and you knew that something special was about to happen. No matter who might find our little foursome strange, he would make them accept us. Where he went, a celebration happened. No one hated us when Bang Bang was there. I've always said, where Bang Bang goes, Pride follows."

"Who's the other guy?" I asked, unsure of what else I could say to my Uncle. "The one sitting with Bang—Morty?"

"Robert," Vic answered.

"I've never met him," I said. "Is he...is he coming tonight?"

It seemed an odd question, considering how old he looked in a photo twenty-five years old.

"If Bang Bang is coming, so is Robert," Uncle Vic said.

"Cool," I responded, turning to him. "Knowing Bang Bang, that'll be around midnight, right?"

Vic's eyes twinkled mischievously as he opened his mouth to respond. Doorbell chimes made him stop and turn away to glance down toward the entryway.

'Finally!' Uncle Harry's voice carried from the kitchen.

Uncle Vic raised his arm to glance at his watch.

An honest to goodness watch.

"Five-fifty-eight." He winked at me. "Thank goodness."

"Go on." I waved him off as Harry's footsteps thundered from the living room. "Intercept before he snatches the wig off of the caterer."

"How right you are." He sighed with a grin, then stepped past me to hurry down the hall.

Uncle Vic reached the front door just a moment before Uncle Harry exited the living room into the entryway, looking loaded for bear. Of course, the caterer had arrived before the time they had told Vic on the phone, but Harry wasn't pleased either way. Having them arrive just an hour before the party was unacceptable, regardless of whether or not an hour was plenty of time for them to set up. Harry had his expectations—realistic or not—and if they weren't met, everyone would hear about it. I watched with amusement as Vic took a moment to settle Harry down in the entryway. Then the door was swung wide, and catering staff was rushing in with trays and containers and serving implements.

I stepped to the side, allowing them to rush by me in the hall on their way to the kitchen. Some of the staff were carrying containers with steam coming from them, while others looked as though they had just been removed from a refrigerator. More staff spilled through the door carrying cases of beer and other beverages. At least one of the employees was carrying a box full of liquor bottles—mostly vodka and tequila from what I could tell, though I saw a few bottles that contained darker liquids. My back stayed against the wall as at least a dozen of the caterer's people rushed past me, on a mission to make a party happen in an hour. As soon as all of the staff had dropped things off in the kitchen, they raced back down the hallway—in a professional manner, of course—to go out and retrieve more trays and containers from the caterer's vehicles out front.

The next round consisted of giant vessels—almost like horse troughs really—being carried down the hallway. An employer at either end, the troughs were brought down the hall, and more boxes and containers followed. The third trip consisted of giant bags of ice and salt being carried along the hall as I held my position against the wall and out of the way. Harry and Vic were carrying on a conversation with the owner of the catering business in the entryway, staying clear of the open doorway. When the employees came through the house on what I assumed was the final trip, catering equipment and devices in tow, Harry began to shout orders, ignoring the conversation that continued between Vic and the caterer.

"*Beers in one and sodas, waters in the other. Ice them down good, people! We need them nice and cold for everyone at seven o'clock! The extra ice can go in the deep freeze through the door off of the kitchen in the garage!*" He commanded.

"*Get the chafing dishes set up, guys!*" The caterer followed up. "*Keep the cold items covered and in the fridge until six-forty. Then we'll get everything set up on ice!*"

"*Is twenty minutes enough?*" I heard Harry ask urgently, turning to the caterer.

Uncle Vic caught my eye from the other end of the hall and gave me a sly wink as the caterer and Harry launched into another animated discussion. Sounds of the catering staff banging around in the kitchen sounded through the house as I pushed away from the wall, returning Vic's wink. There wasn't a particular secret language Uncle Vic and I shared, but we always amused ourselves pretending that Harry exasperated us. The wall of photos in front of me got a final lingering glance, then I made my way down the hall towards the kitchen.

Ignoring what was going on in the entryway was easy once I got to the other end of the house. Not only did Vic and Harry have a large house, but the clamor coming from the kitchen, thanks to the catering staff, blocked out anything else. I peered through the kitchen doorway, giving myself a moment to watch the staff work together to get things set up. Bodies glided to and fro in the kitchen, a symphony of well-trained and highly skilled staff working in synchronicity to achieve one goal. I'd worked in kitchens, even spent time as a waiter for a catering company in New York, when I was in my late teens and early twenties, so I wasn't unfamiliar with the way things were supposed to work. The Littleburg Rainbow Catering Company put all others to shame, even the ones in big cities.

Not that I'd ever been invited to such prestigious events, but I had a feeling that The Littleburg Rainbow Catering Company could teach a thing or two to the folks who catered the Met Gala. I'd never received an invitation, of course, so that was good enough reason for me to believe they didn't run things well there.

I slipped into the half-bathroom at the end of the hall, just past the kitchen, so that I could look out of the window to see what was going on outside with the catering staff.

Unbeknownst to me, the DJ had arrived, having apparently come around the side of the house to sneak in and start setting up his booth. I watched with rapt attention as he began his work, setting up electronic equipment I didn't recognize, nor would I know how to use even if a gun was placed to my head. Another guy, a little older than the first guy, appeared from around the house, a stack of electronic equipment piled in his arms. Obviously, the DJ had an assistant—or a buddy—to help him get set up for my uncles' party. Telling which guy was the DJ and which one was the assistant was easy. The guy with the jeans covered in rainbow patches, a tank top in a pink so bright it could blind the sun, enough stainless-steel jewelry for a WWE wrestler, and hair so tall it could have lunch with Jesus, was obviously the DJ. The other guy was in simple black jeans and a black t-shirt, dark hair of a natural, God-given color, and simple, yet fashionable kicks. He obviously hadn't come to perform. He was just a friend of the DJ's. Of course, when it came to *A Straight Line,* my uncles didn't want for friends.

Ever since I could remember, my uncles' bar had been a part of my life. Not that I was going to the bar regularly until I was older and happened to be in town, of course, since only people over the age of eighteen were allowed inside, but they'd owned and operated it for my entire life. When I was a little kid, and my parents would bring me to visit my uncles—Uncle Vic is my dad's brother—they'd all be talking about the bar. *How's it doing this year? Making money yet? Don't you worry, running a gay bar out here in the sticks? Really? You made that much this year? We drove by on the way in, and there's a crowd out the door, Vic!*

Sometimes, though I was too young, my parents and my uncles would take me to the bar early in the afternoon to eat. That was after the addition of a bar and grill. After several years of owning the bar, and it had started making enough money, Harry and Vic decided that serving a simple menu for lunch and early supper would help make them even more money. Much to my parents' astonishment, my uncles had invested a lot of their profits into having a kitchen installed at the back of the bar and then had a dining area built onto the building.

After the construction, the local—and not so local— LGBTQ-plus people could stop by for a burger and fries, a sandwich and chips, simple pasta dishes, wings, and the typical things you'd see on the menu at a similar establishment. I always loved the chicken fingers and coleslaw. The bar and grill was a success, often frequented by LGBTQ-plus and not so LGBTQ-plus people in Littleburg and the surrounding area. It was good, affordable, and a lot of fun. Eventually, on Fridays, Bang Bang organized it so that all of the local drag performers came in and performed wait staff duties, cracking jokes, cackling uproariously with patrons, and slinging hash. All of the tips they made went to charity.

The money went to LGBTQ-plus charities, the cancer center a few towns over, the homeless shelter, and the soup kitchen. Many of kids at Littleburg Elementary got new books and learning supplies in their classrooms, thanks to Bang Bang's brilliant idea. Of course, this only helped normalize *A Straight Line's* existence in the community and endeared Harry, Vic, and Bang Bang to the more uptight members of the community. Honestly, I think that was Bang Bang's primary motivation in starting Drag Queen Dinners—that's what she called them—not so much altruism. Uncle Vic always said that Bang Bang was "one step ahead on the chessboard," and I couldn't help but believe he was right. Some people might think having ulterior motives made Bang Bang conniving. However, people were genuinely helped by Bang Bang's ideas, and her *conniving* was only motivated by wanting more people in the community to accept and respect the LGBTQ-plus community. To me, that's just altruism with a twist.

Meeting Bang Bang for the first time was quite an event in my life, mostly because I had been five-years-old when it happened. Watching a six-foot three-inch tall man in six-inch heels, a sequin gown, a shiny white wig, wearing enough makeup to intimidate a clown, and a smile made out of pearly white teeth, walk towards you is shocking for any five-year-old. I remember standing at Uncle Vic's side, my little hand in his, my face turned and pressed against his leg, with one eye just uncovered enough to watch the approaching Bang Bang. She looked like a giant cartoon coming towards me.

Russy, this is Bang Bang Baisemoi.

My face turned marginally so that I could see Bang Bang kneel down, her hands coming to rest on her knees as she brought her face somewhat level with mine. She smiled brilliantly, her warmth radiating like the sun, and I couldn't help but wonder how someone could perch so easily in the shoes she was wearing. At the time, I wasn't sure if I was meeting a man or woman, but even in my five-year-old brain, I knew this woman was pretty big for a woman—or anyone really.

Russy. It's nice to meet you.

She held her perfectly manicured hand out to me. It only took a few false starts over the moments that followed, but I eventually shook her hand.

I think that maybe…you need some chocolate.

Upon uttering those words, Bang Bang had endeared my five-year-old self to her immediately. Whenever I was visiting my uncles in the years that followed, if Bang Bang was around, I was following her like a lost puppy.

Of course, I was much older—older than I would like to admit—before I realized "Bang Bang Baisemoi" basically meant *"Bang Bang Fuck Me."* That's just not something a five-year-old will figure out on their own, and it's not a joke adults tend to explain to children.

Thinking about Bang Bang performing at Harry's and Vic's last hurrah made me smile as I stared absently out of the bathroom window and watched the DJ, his assistant, and the catering staff work. As I grew older, the trips to visit my uncles had gotten less frequent—being a teenager, and eventually, a college student, took up a lot of my time—but I always managed to get to *A Straight Line* to see Bang Bang perform at least once when I did visit. One more chance to see her do her thing for the bar made me feel the closest to happy I'd been in a long time.

Two things happened at once that drew my attention from the activities in the backyard. The front doorbell rang, and there was a murmuring in the kitchen. I pulled my face away from the window when I heard Uncle Harry greeting someone loudly, wondering who had arrived. Was it the columnist from *The Gazette?* The murmuring in the kitchen, however, drew my attention more. It sounded like a hushed disagreement, which meant that the catering staff might have encountered a problem. If Harry and Vic were busy with whoever was ringing the doorbell, they probably hadn't noticed the disturbance in the kitchen. The person, or people, at the door would be distracting them anyway, so they wouldn't have time to deal with a problem.

I pushed away from the window, giving the guy in the black t-shirt and jeans a final look, and made my way out of the bathroom. As I walked the few steps from the half-bathroom towards the kitchen, I glanced down the hall. Uncle Vic and Uncle Harry were leading a woman in a skirt and a sensible top with a blazer thrown over it into the living room. *Columnist, obviously.* I smiled to myself and hooked a left into the kitchen. What I encountered was not catering staff in a disagreement about what went where or when or how to set up the buffet.

Phil and Simon, two of my uncles' oldest—and cattiest—friends were standing by the kitchen island where a large tray of canapes was displayed. The owner of Littleburg Rainbow Catering Company, the woman Harry and Phil had been talking to when I went to the bathroom, was glaring at Simon. He was leaning into Phil and clasping his hands together and rubbing them, as though they hurt.

Arthritis, maybe?

"Simon, my love," Phil was patting his husband's back, "no means no. Keep your hands off of the food until the party starts."

"*Bitch!*" Simon hissed across the island at the woman.

"You listen to me, Simon Hopseth." She put one hand on her hip and used her other hand to point at him. "If you so much as breathe on this food before Harry and Vic give the go-ahead, I will personally kick your ass from here to Dubuque."

"Now, now," Phil interjected just as Simon leaned forward to hiss once again. "Both of you be nice to each other."

I leaned against the doorjamb, waiting to see how this apparent fight between Simon and the owner of the catering company went. If fur started to fly, I didn't want to be in the middle of it. I had known Simon long enough to know that he was the cattiest queen to ever live, and he was not above ripping a wig or hair extension off of or out of a woman's head. I didn't know the woman who owned the catering company, but from the glare she was aiming at Simon, I was pretty sure that she could hold her own. I'm not a fighter, but I can recognize them.

"What's going on?" I asked blandly.

Simon, Phil, and the woman all looked over at me, apparently having forgotten that they were in someone else's home where anyone could walk up and witness their scene.

"Russy!" Phil beamed.

I returned his smile, but Simon didn't have time for reunions.

"This bitch slapped my hand!" Simon jabbed a thumb over his shoulder at her.

The woman brought herself up to her full height, ready to launch a verbal volley Simon's way. I pushed away from the doorjamb and held a hand up to her with a smile.

"You probably have better things to do," I said. "I can make sure Simon doesn't finger the canapes."

The woman's eyes bore into Simon's a moment longer, then they flicked over to me. With a swift nod, obviously confident that Harry's and Vic's nephew would protect their food, she turned on her heels and marched out the backdoor.

Overseeing the activities in the backyard was more important—and peaceful—apparently.

"Simon." I shook my head.

"I just wanted to sample the food." Simon murmured like a struck puppy as he cradled his hand. "And that *bitch* slapped my hand like Sister Mary Stick-up-her-cooch."

Phil brayed with laughter as Simon did his best impersonation of an abused animal. Without a word, I walked over and wrapped my arms around Phil, giving him my biggest bear hug, then I gave Simon a daintier hug. I didn't want him to accuse me of trying to choke him or something. As I pulled out of the hug, Simon peered over his shoulder at the platter of food once again. I used one arm to corral him towards the kitchen table.

Once I had Simon seated, and he was no longer a threat to the food or the caterer's mental well-being, I relaxed. His partner, Phil, gave me a smile, silently thanking me for intervening before Simon and the caterer came to blows. I wasn't overly familiar with Simon and Phil, but since they'd been together for nearly as long as my uncles had been, and they were friends with them, I'd been around them enough times to consider them something besides strangers. Though, I wouldn't have exactly called them friends if pressed for a label. They were friends of my uncles and, Phil at least, was easy to get along with, so they were fine by me. Simon, on the other hand, could also be a holy terror, as evidenced by the way he spoke to a person catering someone else's party.

"You guys are here early," I said.

I hoped the simple observation would be enough to get a conversation going and to further distract Simon from the events that had transpired moments before.

Simon craned his neck to look up at me. "Dan and Rafi said they were coming early to see if Vic and Harry needed any help. We thought it would be a nice gesture."

Nice gesture. I laughed internally. All of my uncles' friends would show up early so that they could have first dibs at the food and to gossip about everyone as they arrived. It just wasn't a get-together with the elder gays unless a crack was made about everyone's outfit as they stepped into the party. Simon was one of the worst offenders if memory served me well.

"Surprisingly, they haven't made it," I said.

Dan and Rafi not arriving super early to any party Harry and Vic threw was rare. Of course, both of them were slightly older than my uncles, so it was likely they weren't moving as quickly as they once did. They'd probably show up when everyone else did, getting lost in the shuffle.

"That's a shame," Phil said as he laid a hand on Simon's shoulder.

"No bother." Simon fluttered a hand through the air. "Where are your uncles, Russ? They'll obviously need our help since Dan and Rafi couldn't be bothered, and—"

"They're in the living room with the reporter from *The Gazette*." I stopped him. "They're doing that article about themselves and *A Straight Line's* history in the community. So, they're talking to her right now."

Phil smiled.

"Oh, lord." Simon laid a hand to his chest. "I hope Vic is telling the stories. Harry could never weave a yarn to save his—I'm sorry to speak that way about your uncle, Russ, but Harry blathers on about nothing whenever anyone asks him *anything*. We had your uncles over for dinner two weeks ago, and I mentioned that I was thinking about buying new place settings, and—"

"Russ doesn't care, my love." Phil squeezed Simon's shoulder, mercifully putting an end to the blathering Simon was doing.

Simon looked up at Phil for a moment, cross, then looked over at me. With visible difficulty, he smiled.

"Of course," He said, "your uncles probably have a list of things for you to do before the party starts. You don't have time to listen to me."

"I always have time for you, Simon." I decided to be magnanimous. "But you know how Harry is. If I don't stay on top of things, he'll chew me a new one."

Simon and Phil laughed easily, knowing that I was barely being hyperbolic.

"I'll go check on them." I patted Simon's shoulder, then looked at his husband. "Keep this guy out of the food, will you?"

Simon huffed, but Phil gave me an amused smile. My request would be honored by Phil, or at least I felt safe enough to leave the two alone in the kitchen while I ventured to the living room. As I walked back into the hallway, I could hear Simon start hiss-whispering something to Phil. It was probably something catty about how I was dressed or the way I had spoken to him. I hate to use the term "catty old queen" regarding anyone, let alone friends of my uncles, but the term fit perfectly for Simon. When he got into a room with Harry, the cattiness was legendary. Epic poems have been written about the cattiness the two could produce in a single evening.

Actually, it wasn't poems. More like limericks.

Further down the hall, I could hear the voices of my uncles, as well as the noise produced by the catering staff getting things ready outside. The writer from the newspaper was silent, or at least speaking quietly enough that I couldn't hear her. However, from the sounds of things, Harry and Vic were regaling her with a story to answer one of her questions. As I approached the doorway to the living room, down the hallway by the front door, I stopped just shy of stepping out where my uncles and the writer could see me. Instead, I leaned against the wall, just before the doorway, and listened to their conversation. I wasn't necessarily being nosy, but I was curious about what type of questions the writer was asking and how my uncles were answering. Making my presence known would change the way they all behaved.

"*And that's why we started serving fish on Fridays.*" Harry finished whatever story he had just regaled the writer with.

A woman's laughter drifted out of the living room and rang in my ears. Whatever the story had been about, it had obviously been a good one. Since I hadn't heard it, I couldn't comment on the validity of it.

"*You are a delight, Harry.*" The writer giggled. "*I'm so glad I came today.*"

"*We're so glad to have you.*" Vic's voice reached my ears.

"*Thank you,*" She replied, "*Now, what was it like being the first—and only—gay bar in the area? I mean, this was in the 80s, and—*"

"*Nineteen-eighty.*" Vic clarified. "*Summer of, to be a little more precise.*"

"*Right.*" The writer agreed. "*That must have been a difficult time to open up a gay bar in…well, in such a rural area, right?*"

"*Let me tell you.*" Harry groaned.

"*You've done it now.*" Vic chuckled.

More giggles from the writer.

"*Well strap one on, missy,*" Harry began, making me cover my mouth to stifle a laugh, "*because as soon as we made our intentions known to the City Council, the County Clerk, and the Secretary of State—to get our license, you know—not to mention the ABD—we were given trouble. This had to be inspected. That had to be inspected. Then we needed a final inspection. Paperwork got lost, shuffled around—*"

"*Most people were at least respectful, though,*" Vic added. "*Even if begrudgingly. Most of the officials did their jobs, mind you.*"

"*Yes, well,*" Harry said, "*they still gave us the run-around the best they could when they could. We were a week from opening before we were given the green flag to get things moving. Then the assholes told us that we'd have a* final *inspection the day before we opened. I tell you—*"

"*I'm sure it's a standard thing,*" Vic added diplomatically.

"*Well,*" Harry said, almost out of breath from the frenzy he was whipping himself into, "*we worked night and day that final week, and had just finished sweeping the floor when the inspector showed up. He did all he could to find something wrong, but Vic, Bang Bang, and I—Bang Bang Baisemoi, our star drag performer?—well, we had done everything perfectly. He couldn't find enough to fail us, so we were given the go-ahead. Showed that sonofabitch, didn't we, Vic?*"

"He was just being thorough," Vic added diplomatically once more.

"Oh, screw that." Harry sniped. *"He wanted to fail us so bad I could smell it on him. But there wasn't anything to fail us for, and he had to give us the thumbs up. So, on a Thursday evening at six o'clock, we found out that Bang Bang would be putting butts in the seats the following night as planned."*

"Wow." The writer gasped. *"That's a close call."*

"I should say," Harry replied. *"But we had our bar, we had the green light, and we had each other. We sat down and had a drink to celebrate. The three of us were happier than pigs in shit."*

"I can imagine." The writer responded.

"Then a goddamn brick came through the window," Harry growled. *"Completely shattered the front window. The one you can still see under the awning by the front door? Shattered it into a million pieces. Well, we all jumped up, raced to the door—once we got over being startled, of course—and saw a pickup speeding away, tires squealing."*

I waited to hear Vic correct Harry, but he said nothing. The reporter was quiet as well.

"Well, as you can imagine," Harry said, *"we were fit to be tied. There we were, feeling like celebrating the fact that we'd get to open on time, and our damned front window is in pieces."*

"Oh my gosh." The reporter gasped. *"That's awful!"*

"Tell me about it," Harry said, *"But the three of us pooled the last bit of energy we had, drove over to the nearest hardware store down there in, uh, in—"*

"Cedar Rapids." Vic offered.

"—Cedar Rapids," Harry continued, *"and got the glass and things we'd need to fix it. When we got back, we patched that window up good as new. We didn't get to bed until well after midnight, but A Straight Line made its debut the following night. Homophobes be damned!"*

Silence filled the house. The catering staff clamored outside.

"That's quite a story." The reporter finally responded. *"I didn't know that part of the bar's history."*

"Well," Harry said, *"a lot of people don't know all we went through to bring a safe place to the LGBTQ-plus community around here. But we did it. And we're proud that, forty years later, we're passing it off into capable hands that will continue its legacy."*

Before I knew it, the interview was coming to an end—which was a good thing, since the start of the party was nearing—and the reporter was getting up to make her exit. Vic and Harry said their pleasant "thank yous" and "our pleasures," and the reporter said she could see herself out. They all fussed over each other a moment longer, so I took the opportunity to put my back against the wall, hoping the reporter would walk right past me and out the front door. I didn't want the reporter to think I was eavesdropping, though that was essentially what I had been doing. She didn't know I was Harry's and Vic's nephew, so there was no telling what she'd assume.

Fortunately, the reporter did as I had wanted and exited the living room, her back to me as she ambled towards the front door. I was about to breathe a sigh of relief as she opened the door and stepped out of the house. However, at the last second, she turned to close the door behind herself, and her eyes rose, locking with mine. I gave her a weak smile and wave as she stared at me, completely confused, but she carried on her way. The door shut, and she was gone, and I was left to push away from the wall and step around the doorjamb into the living room.

Harry and Vic were on the couch, talking to each other quietly, looking happy to have a moment to themselves when I entered the room. I almost turned around and left the same way I entered, just so they could have a few more moments of peace, but realized that would just look strange if they looked up and saw me leaving. So, I stood there, waiting for them to notice me. It didn't take long before Harry looked up at me, a smile on his face.

"That bitch Simon in the kitchen?" He asked.

I laughed. "Yeah. Phil's watching him."

"I heard his shrill little voice the moment he stepped in the back door," Harry said. "All the way across the damn house, at that."

"Harry." Vic shook his head admonishingly, though the curve at the corner of his mouth betrayed him. "Be nice to our guests tonight."

"If I must." Harry waved him off as his eyes came to rest on mine once more. "What are you doing, Russ?"

"Just waiting on you guys to get done and tell me what to do to help." I shrugged. "I never heard that story about the brick coming through the window at the bar before. Why didn't—"

"Because," Simon's voice chimed from behind me, "he told it wrong."

We all turned to find Simon standing in the doorway between the dining room and living room, hands on his hips, lips pursed, and Phil looking over his shoulder apologetically.

"I didn't tell it wrong," Harry grumbled from behind me.

"It was barely a rock." Simon jabbed a finger at Harry. "I may not have been there when it happened, but Bang Bang showed me the evidence. A *brick?* You're either forgetting details due to old age, or you're making them up to sound like you're actually interesting."

For the briefest, but tensest of moments, the room grew quiet. We all stood there in awkward, bated silence as we waited for the two biggest queens in the room to bare their claws and have at each other. With what I knew about my uncle and Simon, it wouldn't have surprised me in the slightest if they actually struck each other before it was all said and done. Of course, I would have helped pull them apart—played my role in things—but I wouldn't have been shocked at having to do it. Harry and Simon were cut from the same cloth, which was probably why the two of them were always at odds.

"Well, Simon," Harry chirped from behind me, "it's so brave of you to show up, what with that ghastly rumor going around about you!"

"What?" Simon's eyes widened. "Which rumor?"

"I haven't decided yet," Harry stated simply.

I had to bite my bottom lip to chase away the wicked grin my brain so desperately wanted to plaster all over my face. Phil was doing his best to choke back laughter behind his husband's back. Simon shot an annoyed look over his shoulder at Phil, then turned back to glare at Harry.

"Clever little Mary, aren't you?" Simon spat.

"Are you here for the free food or to bring down property values, Simon?" Harry groaned, signaling that he was rising from the couch. "Not that I haven't seen you multitask before, of course."

"That's what you do?" Simon mumbled. "Insult the guests who come over early to help you finish setting up for your party?"

"Oh, calm down," Harry said as he stepped past me, on his way to join his friends, "of course, we're so happy to see the both of you. Maybe Phill more than you, Simon, but we're happy nonetheless. It was very kind of the both of you to come early to help with the final preparations."

"I should say so." Simon snipped. "Wait. You're being nice. Did you get the cancer or something? It's too late to get into Heaven, you old bitch."

Uncle Harry barked with laughter as he wrapped an arm around each of his friends' shoulders, his head shaking slightly upon his neck as he turned them back towards the kitchen. In a murmur of questions and accusations, as well as answers and denials, the three of them made their way back into the kitchen, suddenly leaving me in silence once the door swung shut lazily behind them. It wasn't until I heard Uncle Vic shift behind me that I remembered I wasn't left entirely alone. I turned back to him to find him rising from the couch as well, managing with less of a grimace, and much less noise, than Harry.

"Vic," I said, "I never heard that story about the brick—*or rock*—coming through the window at the bar."

"You didn't, did you?" He said, his hands sliding over his pants to smooth out the wrinkles they'd gathered while sitting for the interview.

"So?"

Vic looked up at me, consternation etched all over his face.

"It wasn't a brick," He said.

"So, Uncle Harry—"

"And it wasn't a rock." Vic waved me off. "It was a cinderblock. And it was on fire. I suspect they doused it in gasoline or kerosene before chucking it through the window. It's possible that the perpetrators hung around long enough to spew a few choice words through the gaping hole it left. We may even know who did it. Got a good look at his face through the hole in the window, after all. Word got around, and rumors flew in the community—you know how us queers can conflate drama—so Bang Bang found a rock and started showing it to people. She played it down a bit so people wouldn't worry about coming to the bar."

"We've all had rocks thrown at us. Fists. Bottles. Whatever," Vic said. "A cinderblock on fire, well that was new. Bang Bang didn't want anyone to be afraid to come to the bar. She didn't want *A Straight Line* to fail before it had a chance. So, she changed some details to make it a little less startling. That's all."

The two of us stared at each other for several moments, the weight of the true story hanging in the air between us. The gravity of what being a queer in small-town America was like.

"Why didn't you tell the police who did it?" I finally asked.

Vic's hand was waving through the air gently again.

"It would have been pointless, Russ," He said. "Besides, if they knew we had a shattered window, that would have led to another inspection before we could open."

Uncle Vic shrugged, then sidestepped to head towards the kitchen and join the rest of the guys.

"But," I stopped him, "did you really all just go to the hardware store, buy supplies, and stay up into the wee hours fixing it?"

"Well," Vic turned to look at me as though I were dense, "of course. The window had to be fixed before we opened."

I frowned at him.

"But why?"

Vic knew what question I was really asking. I wanted to understand how something so startling, so demeaning, so threatening could happen, and their solution was to *not* tell the police and just fix it.

"Because that's what we do, Russ," He said.

"You and Harry and Bang Bang?"

"No." He chuckled. "Us queers. We get called names. We have our rights threatened or taken away. We get beaten. Arrested. Murdered. We get rocks and bricks, and even cinderblocks on fire, hurled at us. Our businesses are attacked. We get ignored and ridiculed when we complain. We get knocked down. But we get back up, and we keep marching. We keep going. It's our duty as queers. We hope that we make a difference for the next generation of queers that follows. For every one of us you manage to win against, ten more will take their place. *We're here, we're queer, we're not going anywhere.*"

Then he winked at me and strode towards the kitchen.

The doorbell rang.

Chapter 3
The Flirtatious Five

Listening to the sound coming from the porch, a cacophony of talking, bickering, and laughing, I could tell who had rung the bell. Vic and Harry didn't come running to answer the door—not that either was known for sprinting unless absolutely necessary—so I took it upon myself to greet the next round of guests. It struck me funny, as I made my way into the foyer to answer the door, how odd Harry's and Vic's friends were. I'd been at their home many times when they threw dinner parties or afternoon barbecues. Everyone always showed up late. There seemed to be a contest to see who could be the most fashionably late queer in all of Littleburg.

If you were to mention that the event they were invited to involved *A Straight Line*, younger gays, food and drinks, not to mention a performance from Bang Bang, they all wanted to be the first ones to arrive. The ruse was that they all wanted to arrive early to "help out," but they all really wanted to see and be seen. Harry's and Vic's friends knew that any major event they put on for the bar attracted media attention—and all the queers in a hundred-mile radius, if not more. There might be a chance to be interviewed by the nightly news or, at least, the newspaper. There'd be young, hot men to ogle. Food and drinks were a given. None of their friends would miss any of it, even if they were sick in the hospital.

I wouldn't have been surprised if someone had an iron lung wheeled into the middle of A Straight Line. *I thought to myself.*

Not to say that Harry and Vic had bad friends or anything. All of their friendships, most of them anyway, had been lifelong. Any of their friends would be there in sickness or loss or happiness and health. They'd just show up twenty or thirty minutes late. That's all.

As the door swung wide, a rainbow of button-down shirts greeted me. Blue, yellow, orange, purple, and green shone out at me. The green shirt, in particular, caught my attention because it was the same color Uncle Harry had chosen. A wicked grin came to my face as a thought entered my head: *Harry will be livid.*

Felix, Frank, Fredrick, Floyd, and Phil—sometimes called *Phil Number Two* so as to not confuse him with Simon's partner—stood on the front porch, clustered together, every single pair of lips flapping wildly.

The Flirtatious Five. That's what they were called by everyone else in the community. It was a moniker Bang Bang had given them decades before, I was told. Of course, that hadn't always set right with Phil. Even though his name started with an "F" sound, it didn't actually start with one. He had wanted to know why they couldn't have a group name that was an alliteration that began with a "P."

Passel of Perverts? Bang Bang had apparently suggested. *The Pestilent Pack? "Pigs" starts with a "P," so maybe—*

In the end, *The Flirtatious Five* moniker had been approved by four of the members with the fifth abstaining from the impromptu vote. Bang Bang had labeled the gang, and the vote had taken place years before I was born, so I had always referred to the group of guys by their collective name as far back as I could remember. It was easier than naming them one by one when greeting them. They all always seemed to be together all of the time anyway.

In fact, no one really seemed to know which members of the group were actually a couple. They'd mingled and dated willy-nilly amongst themselves since the beginning. One week, two of them would be shacking up; the next, there'd be a thruple. Then one would be alone while the other four did their thing. At one point, I think none of them were sure who was supposed to be whose partner. If I had to describe the romantic relationships within the group, I would say it was "fluid." Recently, I'd heard from Vic in a text he'd sent me a few weeks before I'd come to stay with them, that all five guys were now living in the same assisted living facility. It wasn't a nursing home by a long shot, just a block of apartments where seniors lived that had assistance in the form of an on-site nurse, cooking and cleaning staff, and plenty of other amenities. The Flirtatious Five were perfectly capable physically and mentally, but if you can afford to live in a place where people cook and clean for you—and will help you out of your recliner—why not, right?

"Hey, guys," I said.

It took a second, but the bickering and laughing finally tapered off, and all of the guys turned to look at me. Immediately, genuine smiles replaced the scowls they wore for each other, and five pairs of arms were reaching out to pull me in for a hug. At first, I thought that I'd spend quite a bit of time hugging and greeting each of the five, but an awkward group hug ended my worry. All five of the guys started jabbering at me simultaneously so that I couldn't understand one question or greeting, though I got the jist that they were all happy to see me "*after such a long time.*"

Felix, short and slender, a slight gay man who somehow always seemed to command attention and respect, even from brawnier types, took charge.

"Russy," He said, speaking over the rest, "*Russy!* Shut up, you old hags. Russy. Where are your uncles?"

"In the kitchen," I said.

I stepped back, swinging the door wide as I jabbed a thumb over my shoulder.

"You should find them in there with Simon and Phil," I added.

Four of the Flirtatious Five began blathering again as they pushed past me, making their way deeper into the house to find the other four men waiting in the kitchen. Hopefully, they'd all chip in and help Vic and Harry finish any last-minute things for the party, though I knew that Harry and Vic were probably just doing their best to keep Simon out of the food. Felix hung back as his four cohorts squawked and waddled down the long hallway towards the kitchen. Once the rest of the Five were out of the immediate vicinity, Felix's arm found mine, lacing through the crook of my elbow.

Felix was the most flirtatious of the bunch, and I was a younger man. His favorite. But Harry and Vic were my uncles, so he never came on stronger than was funny.

"Now, Russy," He cooed, "please tell me there are other handsome young men here besides yourself. I can't fawn over you all night. Harry and Vic would have my hide. And I'm much too old for you?"

It was a question. Not a statement.

I laughed as I swung the door shut.

"Sorry," I said, "I'm still holding out for Prince Charming."

A lump of heat settled in my stomach. I ignored it.

"A shame." He shook his head, mostly kidding, as I turned us towards the hallway. "I assumed you'd come to your senses one day."

"I guess I'm just hardheaded, Felix." I chuckled as I led us slowly down the hallway.

Felix was favoring his right leg, which let me know that he wasn't getting around as well as he had been the last time I'd seen him. All of the young gay men in Littleburg who had been running from Felix for years would rejoice once word got out.

He patted my hand. "You know I just love to flirt. It's how we—"

"Got the name."

"Exactly," He said. "I could never seriously consider a dalliance with my best friends' nephew, of course."

"Of course." I laughed.

"Now," He asked, "what is that bitch Simon doing here before us? Picking at the food?"

"He's tried," I said. "So far, we've kept him in check, though. It's a four-man operation. He's pretty slick for a feisty old queer."

Felix guffawed as we entered the kitchen, drawing all eyes to us. Harry's eyes darted over from his place keeping court around the island. When his gaze caught sight of Felix's arm draped through mine, he rolled his eyes. Uncle Vic merely smiled at the arrival of the last of the Flirts, obviously concerned that the ringleader had not arrived with the group. Now that I had delivered Felix, the core group of elder gays was together. If Bang Bang was ever at a party on time, the entire group would be together in one place.

The nine guys in the kitchen, and Bang Bang, were the core group of elder gays because they were all of the men still alive who had been at *A Straight Line* on opening night. Whether it was intended or not, that moment in time, the solidarity shown between the gay men on the opening night of a gay bar in bumfuck Iowa had created friendships that had lasted, quite literally, a lifetime. Sure, there had been others who had been part of the group—once upon a time—but they were no longer with us. What was once twenty or thirty guys was now ten. Next-generation gays were replacing the faces you'd see nightly at the bar.

Harry and Vic—and the elder gays—enjoyed seeing younger men around, but they missed the old group. I guess that's one of the side effects of getting older. Your friends start dying.

"I see you didn't bother wearing one of the flag colors." Felix slithered his arm from mine to jab his fists into his hips and admonish Simon.

"What?" Simon perked up.

"A Hawaiian shirt, Si? Really?" Felix shook his head. "At least Phil was queer enough to wear a primary color."

It was true. Simon had arrived in a Hawaiian shirt, and Phil had shown up in a purple shirt—like he had obviously been instructed to do by Harry. Simon never followed the crowd. I suspected that he wanted to stick out in any pictures that showed up on social media. Even older gay men can dream of being Insta-Famous one day, right?

"It's a *summer* party," Simon stated defensively. "It's perfectly acceptable for—"

"He doesn't like blending in." One of the other Flirtatious Five snorted, though I hadn't been quick enough to catch which one it had been.

"Queen." Another voice made my head whip around again.

"Princess at best." Someone quipped, and my head did another spin.

Then the bickering began. I turned to Felix.

"Good job." I teased him as everyone around us began arguing. "You better hope the caterer has everything under control and doesn't need any help because Harry will never get you all focused for long."

Felix snickered.

"Look," He reached into his shirt breast pocket and withdrew a slip of paper, "tell my grandson to make sure at least one of these songs gets played every hour. I don't want to hear Britney and Madonna the *entire* night."

I took the folded slip of paper from him with a frown.

"Your grandson?" I asked.

"I spread my seed far and wide in my younger years, Russy."

"Gross, Felix."

He cackled.

"He's out there at the DJ booth." He explained. "He's helping out tonight."

"That's nice of him," I responded neutrally.

"Yes, yes." He waved me off. "Just make sure he knows to play some of those songs. And tell Denny that if he doesn't, well, my foot doesn't work as well as it should, but it will still manage to find his ass. Comprenez-vous?"

"Got it."

Felix pulled away from me and entered the fray around the island. *Once more into the breach!* So, I turned on my heels and ignored the sound of nine elder gays bickering with each other about who had or hadn't worn the right shirt. Hand delivering a list of songs to someone seemed like a much easier task than trying to corral the men in the kitchen. It would be nearly impossible to make any of them focus on the few last-minute things that needed to be done for the party, so finding Denny was a task I would gladly complete.

When I stepped out the door back onto the Bluestone patio, I could immediately hear the caterer barking orders to the catering staff. They were having an impromptu meeting on the gazebo where they could have some shade. It never got too hot in Littleburg, but the sun beating down on you is still rather warm when you're trying to work. Find shade where you can get it in summer, I suppose. As I thought about that, I realized that maybe I *had* worn the wrong outfit for the outdoor party. I'd been working from home in New York and rarely got to see daylight. Wearing a short-sleeve shirt and shorts might have been better. Soak up some rays. Get a bit of a tan.

Of course, when your cave-dwelling induced lily-white skin hasn't seen the sun in so long, you have to be careful. With the sun beating down on me as I traversed the porch, I already knew I was going to get a sunburn before the day was over. Luckily, with the party starting at seven, there would maybe be an hour or hour-and-a-half where the sun would have its way with me. Maybe I'd escape a burn if I was lucky.

The DJ—Denny, I presumed—was jamming cables into different pieces of equipment and hooking up his laptop when I approached. My first impression of him was that he looked absolutely nothing like his grandfather. Felix was a handsome man and had held onto his looks pretty well through the years. Denny was not exactly what anyone would call a "stunner." Of course, I'm nothing special to look at myself, so

I don't judge others by their looks. Denny's appearance was merely an observation. His grandfather was handsome. He was not. Of course, genetics don't work in a way that makes grandsons resemble their grandfathers often, so it was pointless to consider for long.

"Hey," I said as I approached, the list of songs in hand, "your grandfather asked me to ask you to play these songs. He doesn't want to hear Britney and Madonna all night—his words, not mine. I would have said different artists' names since I actually live in this century, but—"

"Who?" Denny's brow creased as he pulled his eyes away from the equipment to meet my gaze.

"Oh, I'm Russ." I smiled, offering my hand. "Sorry."

Denny took my hand and gave it a tentative shake.

His hands were sweaty.

"No," He said, "who told you to give me the list?"

"Felix," I said, sliding my hand from his, "your grandfather."

"Well," He reached up to rub the back of his neck with his sweaty hand, "my grandfather is dead, so you might have the wrong guy."

"What?" I laughed nervously. "Felix said his grandson Denny was DJing and—"

"I'm not Denny," He said. "I'm Denny's roommate. Bird."

I stared at him. With his hairdo and the bright pink of his shirt, "Bird" was appropriate.

"Caw. Caw." He flapped his arms gently. "Bird."

"That's—that's a name." I chuckled.

He shrugged.

Ooookay.

"Well, Felix told me to tell Denny about the song list," I continued, "so, I guess you're helping Denny with the DJ equipment, or…?"

"Nah," Bird said, reaching out to take the list from me, "I'm the DJ. Denny's helping me."

"Oh."

"This is a lot of disco." He smirked to himself as he read over the list. "But I have them all. I play a lot of weddings and shit. He wants just these played?"

"Oh." I shook my head to clear it. "No. I mean, I guess play whatever you were intending to play, but mix those songs in with them. The elder gays want to hear some classics, ya' know?"

"Who doesn't love the classics?" Bird agreed.

"Right. Well, thanks, Den—I mean, Bird."

"You're welcome." He smiled, then his eyes flicked to the side of the house. "There's Denny."

I turned just in time to see the actual Denny round the corner of the house, a large plastic milk crate dangling from his hand at his side. Apparently, I had been a bit confused when I saw the two guys setting up the DJ booth. But just a little. The guy behind the booth, setting up the equipment, was obviously the DJ. That had been proven. The guy in the black jeans and t-shirt and fresh kicks was his assistant. However, the assistant hadn't just pitched in to be nice. He was the grandson of one of The Flirtatious Five. Of course, Denny was Felix's grandson. Bird was Denny's roommate. Was Bird DJing free of charge?

Maybe they were both helping out?

"That's what they called me in school." The guy in black—Denny—quipped, a broad grin on his face.

He rounded the booth and set the plastic milk crate behind his roommate. Bird took no interest in Denny or the milk crate. He simply slipped the list of songs under his computer so that it wouldn't blow away, but so he could still read it, then went back to setting up his equipment. I should have been offended that he was no longer interested in anything going on around him—since I was one of those things—but having the music ready for the party was essential.

"Are you looking for me?" Denny asked, rounding the booth once more to approach me.

"Not anymore," I explained. "Your grandfather—Felix—asked me to bring a list of songs out here to you. I guess

I just assumed since he wanted you to have the list that you were Bird and—we've never met before, so…"

As I babbled on, Denny's smile grew, only stopping once I trailed off.

"I'm Denny." He held his hand out. "Felix is my grandfather. I am *not* the DJ."

"I worked most of that out." I took his hand and gave it a shake.

His palms were dry and cool. Denny was obviously a guy with whom summer agreed.

"Grandpa is a little puissant. He likes to think he is, anyway." Denny laughed.

"Great word," I said.

"Your name isn't Noah Webster, is it?" He teased.

"Russ," I said, "writer. Well, it pays the bills."

"That makes perfect sense then," He said, "writers and Noah Webster absolutely adore my vocabulary. I don't mean to brag, but I actually won my fourth-grade spelling bee. In Mrs. Hepstein's class. The competition was tough, but I crushed those nineteen other eight-year-olds like the cockroaches they were."

"So…you didn't make many friends in elementary school, I take it?" I quipped.

"You wouldn't think eight-year-olds could be such sore losers, right?"

I laughed. Bird pushed a cord in somewhere that made the speakers pop. I jumped. Denny didn't.

"*Deus Vult, motherfucker,*" Bird mumbled.

I glanced over at him, somewhat appalled, but also impressed.

"You both seem to have impressive vocabularies," I said.

"He's harmless." Denny waved in the direction of Bird, as though shooing away, well, maybe a bird? "Who do you belong to?"

"I'm sorry?" I asked.

"You belong to one of the other Five?" He asked. "I've never met you, and I think I've met all of their kids and grandkids, and—"

"Russ," I repeated. "I'm Harry's and Vic's nephew."

Denny slapped a hand to his forehead.

"Of course!" He rolled his eyes comically. "I've heard so much about you over the years. Grandpa talks about you. The Flirtatious Five talk about you. *Russy, Russy, Russy.* Harry and Vic are always going on about you."

"Oh?"

"I'm from back west." Denny continued, his hands in perpetual motion. "I guess we were always visiting in summer at different times, and at the holidays, well, it's not like we would've seen each other then. But I've heard a ton about you over the years. I should have figured that's who you were when I saw you. You kind of favor Harry."

"Vic's my biological uncle," I said simply.

"Just in the eyes. That twinkle." He corrected himself. "I wasn't talking about his height."

I chuckled.

"Well," I shrugged, "I guess some things rub off on you?"

"For sure."

Denny continued to smile at me as we stood there, facing each other with not much else to say. Bird was shuffling things around, organizing his booth, ignoring us still. Gazing into Denny's eyes, I didn't like what I saw. Handsome face. Dark hair and eyes. Eyes that a person could fall into and never find their way out. Denny definitely favored Felix. Out of the corner of my eye, I could see that the caterer and her minions were marching away from the gazebo towards the house. I didn't want to pull my phone out to check the time right in front of Denny—it could have been perceived as rude—so I settled for looking up at the sky, as though a human sundial.

"Well," I said, "I guess I should get back inside. I'm sure Harry and Vic will have a few things for me to do."

"Right, right." Denny grinned. "Well, uh, I'll save a dance for you."

I managed to keep a neutral expression on my face, though the proposition bothered me for various reasons.

"Great," I said. "Uh, see you guys later on."

Waving over my shoulder, I turned on my heels and strode back towards the house, hoping I wasn't marching away like I was going off to war—or that I was trying to get away. However, Denny was too good looking and far too charming—if not a bit awkward—for me to tolerate for long. I needed space. And air. Something in my gut was flip-flopping, and I didn't like it. When I entered the house, the caterer and her staff were shooing the elder gays out of the house. Apparently, they had everything under control. *We'll get the door and greet the guests*, the caterer announced loudly over Harry's protestations.

Once the elder gays started being herded towards the back door, I slipped into the hallway to avoid being corralled with everyone else. Being shoved into the pack and stuffed through the doorway would do nothing for my nerves—or my suddenly racing pulse. So, I once again found myself standing in the empty hallway, staring at the memories on the wall. Staring at the pictures Harry and Vic had taken and hung over the years always calmed my nerves. A few minutes to reflect quietly on the history of my uncles and their bar was just what I needed to slow my heart rate and catch my breath. I needed a moment of silence before everyone started arriving for the party.

I don't know how long I stood there, alone, staring at the pictures on display, but it could have only been minutes. None of the staff had made their way to the front door—which I had a clear view of from my position—to watch for party attendees. When Vic popped out of the doorway to the kitchen, glancing around with concern, I knew that he was looking for me. I just gave him a small smile before turning my eyes back to the pictures. Vic stood there for a moment, observing me, an understanding we always had passing between us silently.

"You know," He finally broke the silence, "the DJ booth is kind of new to us. Sure, we have a DJ at the bar three nights a week now—gotta get butts out of seats and on the dance floor, after all—but when the bar opened, we weren't that fancy."

"Yeah?"

"Well, maybe a little fancy for the time," Vic said, "We had a *1980 Rock-Ola Max Jukebox*. Three plays for a quarter. Two bucks would have you dancing all night. It held one-hundred and sixty vinyl records—fancy as hell for a little gay bar in the middle of nowhere in 1980, let me tell you."

I smiled as I stared at a picture of Vic and Harry in San Francisco with Alcatraz off in the distance behind them.

"It came in handy the night that cinderblock came through the window," Vic continued. "Patching things up and cleaning up all the mess wasn't nearly as bad with the *Village People* and *Sister Sledge* playing in the background."

"You're so old, Vic." I teased.

"Well, you've never been a liar," He said, "just a bit of a snot."

I laughed as my eyes drifted over to a picture of Harry, Vic, Bang—*Morty*—and...Robert? They were all on a pontoon boat. Possibly on the Mississippi. The river was too big to be the Wapsipinicon.

"Morty met Robert that night," Vic said, seeing where my eyes had landed. "Did you know that? Of course, not. You never really even met Robert. Anyway, that night, a fiery cinderblock wasn't the one thing that showed up at the bar."

"Robert?"

"Yes," Vic said, "we had finished up repairing the window, and we were cleaning up. Night had settled in, but we had the front door open so we could enjoy the cool air. That probably wasn't the smartest decision, all things considered. Some hillbilly throws a fiery cinderblock through your window—just leave the door open for the next guy, right?"

I laughed nervously.

"But it wasn't another backward thinking homophobe who came through the door. It was Robert. He was driving from Minneapolis to St. Louis that night. Traveling salesman. The last of a dying breed, Russ."

"*You are old,*" I mumbled.

Vic ignored me. "Tall, dark, handsome, but a bit older than the rest of us. He seemed ancient at the time. Time means nothing when you're relatively young. Well, he had been driving that night, and when he got to Littleburg, *A Straight Line* was the only place with a light on. And he was desperately in need of a place to…do some business."

A chuckle escaped my throat.

"Well, Morty recognized him as queer immediately. I think so, anyway." Vic smiled. "I'm pretty sure they spent the night together. None of my business, of course, but as a queer, I have to respect the hell out of two men jumping on an opportunity like that."

"*Get it, Morty,*" I said.

Vic smiled. "After that night, Robert got to Littleburg as often as he could—in between deals, of course. After a time, he decided that he needed to find a job nearby where he wouldn't have to travel so much. And he and Morty became inseparable. A greater, more sordid love story's never been told before. You know, Morty was not one to be locked down in his younger years. He had a new guy at least once a week. Once Robert came into the picture? Forget about it. His days began and ended with that man. It was sweet. All of us guys could hope for something that wonderful."

I just stood there doing anything but looking at my uncle.

"Having someone to call your own—whatever that looks like—is human, Russ," Vic said quietly. "There's nothing wrong with finding someone who is your first and last thing each day."

"Vic—"

"Now," He interjected, "it doesn't have to be traditional. There are all kinds of ways to love and have a relationship. But it's fairly human to want someone to spend your days—hopefully, your life—with. We should never give up on finding it."

I turned to him.

"Look, Vic," I said, "I get it. Just…not right now. Not tonight. Give me some time to stay with you guys before you get all Grandfather Wisdom on me, okay?"

"I worry about you." He placed his hands on my shoulders. "You're my only nephew. The closest thing I'll ever have to a son."

"I'm rather fond of you myself." I teased. "I just need time. All right?"

Vic stared into my eyes, watching me carefully, as though he could see the damage buried deep as if it were a visible thing.

"Fucking men." He sighed, his hands sliding away from my shoulders.

"Fucking men." I parroted.

"Just don't give up hope," He said. "Promise me that. I'm old, Russ. Knowing you'll have someone to look after—and who will look after you—will bring me a bit of peace. It'll make putting up with your uncle so much easier."

I laughed. "I'll do my best."

"You always do." He chucked me under the chin lightly with a grin.

For a moment longer, we stood there, just sharing a look and the silence—the only silence we'd have for hours.

"Shall we join the hens outside?" He asked.

"You go ahead." I gave him a slight nudge. "I'll be out there in a minute. Promise."

"All right," He said. "I'll send Felix and Simon after you if you try and drag it out."

I gasped playfully.

Vic chuckled at my theatrics, but then he was gone. I was left with the sound of the catering staff bustling through the house for background noise as I stared at the picture of Morty and Robert.

Fucking men.

Chapter 4
Boogie Shoes & Chicken Wings

"*Did I ever tell you about the time I met John Travolta in Mykonos?*" Simon was practically screaming his question when I stepped out onto the patio where the elders had gathered.

In the few minutes that had passed between the time I had been outside to talk to Denny and Bird and I had been inside to, essentially, stare at the wall, patio chairs had been drug out of the garage for the elders. Uncle Harry and Uncle Vic were seated in their matching grasshopper green metal Crosley lawn chairs out in the yard—looking every bit the older couple—and a few of the others were in canvas strap lawn chairs of varying colors. It appeared as though the patio was going to also be used for dance floor space. From my experience of staying with my uncles before, I knew that all of the lawn chairs were normally kept in the garage. In fact, they had more lawn chairs than they had sense. Dozens, to be exact. When you entertain outside a lot, I guess having dozens of lawn chairs is a good idea. Regardless, I hadn't retrieved them, and I hadn't seen the catering staff do the job, so I began to worry. Having men in their late 60s and 70s—a few even nearing 80—dragging lawn chairs around in summer was a bad idea. The last hurrah for *A Straight Line* didn't need to start with heat stroke or heart attacks.

"No." I heard a voice echo back from the garage. "You never told me that, Simon."

A quick survey of the area led me to realize that Denny was nowhere in sight. Further deduction led me to realize that he was the person who had fetched the lawn chairs and was currently retrieving more.

"Well," Simon screamed again to be heard over all of the other elders jabbering away amongst themselves, "I went to Mykonos years ago—"

"Mykonos in summer?" Felix piped up. "How original of you, Simon dear."

"We're queers," Simon quipped, "it's what we do. Anyway, I was there years ago. Now, mind you, this was just a few years after *Saturday Night Fever* had come out, and Johnny boy was still a hot commodity. Wouldn't touch him now for money, mind you, but—"

"Or he wouldn't touch you," Felix added.

Simon shot a sideways glance at Felix but didn't let it stop him. "Well, I just so happened to be high as giraffe pussy and completely shit-faced—and I may have been behind a seafood restaurant, reintroducing my insides to the outside—and I just happened to bump into none other than John Travolta himself."

"That's crazy." Denny's voice carried from the garage.

I shuffled across the porch to join the elders who were standing on the lawn, waiting on chairs.

"What in the fuck was John Travolta doing behind a seafood restaurant in Mykonos? Especially when he was one of the most famous faces on the planet?" One of the Five asked.

"Old Queen." Simon waved the question off. "Looking for trade, of course. Rough or otherwise, doesn't matter."

"He found the rough kind." Felix side-eyed Simon. "If anything about you was worth paying for."

"Anyway," Simon barked at Felix, "the point is, I went behind the restaurant to puke my guts up and ended up having them stirred around by none other than Danny Zuko."

"*Bullshit!*" Several of the others barked in disbelief.

Denny's laughter carried from the garage.

"Fuck every last one of you," Simon said, matter-of-factly, "It was one of the greatest moments of my queer existence. Best night of my life."

"And it's been all downhill for the last forty years." Felix quipped, then turned to my uncles. "Do the caterers not serve drinks around here?"

"Help yourself, you old bitch." Harry sat forward in his lawn chair as he jabbed a finger over at the troughs filled with iced down beverages. "We didn't pay a caterer so you could stay off your feet."

"Wouldn't be the first person to accept money for that job." One of the Five quipped, making all the others roar with laughter. I couldn't help but chuckle at the joke myself, though Felix was one of my favorites of the elders.

"I have *never* paid for trade," Felix said. "How utterly common."

"There's no shame in doing what you have to do to get your needs met. And boys have to make a living, Felix," Phil shrugged.

"My point exactly." Felix sat back in his chair and gestured grandly at Phil. "Look at that beard. Some queers will let any old raggedy thing sit on their face."

Again, the elders roared with laughter, even Phil. That was the thing about the elder gays. They lived for their absolutely soul-crushing quips about each other. However, even the butts of the jokes knew it was all in good fun. Due to my time at my uncles' house over the years, I'd learned one thing that I believed above all else. True friends roast the fuck out of each other. And no one gets that offended.

"Hey," Phil replied, "times are rough. So, the trade must be, too."

Again, more cackling from the Peanut Gallery.

"Okay, okay, okay," Denny announced as he exited the side door of the garage, three canvas lawn chairs swinging from each hand. "Don't get yourselves too worked up. None of you have the heart for it anymore."

Denny sauntered over and let the remaining standing elders choose lawn chairs from the selection so they could have a seat.

"I may not have the heart, but I've got the imagination and desire." Simon looked over at Denny and patted his chest right over his heart.

"Checking to see if the Viagra you brought is still in your pocket, Si?" Uncle Harry snipped. "It's still there. It's been there since nineteen-ninety-seven for God's sake. It's as useless as that thing between your legs."

The elders were laughing hysterically once again. Denny stood there, now empty-handed, smiling down at the elders as they formed a semi-circle of lawn chairs to continue their little roasting session. Once they'd all been thoroughly scorched, they'd move on to judging party attendees as they arrived. For now, they only had each other to pick on, and they were perfectly content with that. I just hoped that none of them would turn their quips towards me. Of course, being the nephew of Harry and Vic had some perks, one of which being that none of their friends were ever too catty towards me. It was a surefire way to not get invited to the next party, after all.

"Denny, love," Felix piped up, "are there more chairs in the garage?"

"Of course, there are." Harry scoffed. "We weren't expecting everyone to just stand around forever. Or sit in the grass."

Felix rolled his eyes but kept any comment he had to himself.

"Yeah," Denny said. "Quite a few. Want me to bring them out?"

"Please," Felix beamed up at his grandson. "But first, would you fetch me a drink? Harry is being a terrible host and—"

"I'll get you a drink," I said, wanting something to do besides be the wallflower of the party, "Would anybody else like one?"

Nine elder gays all voiced their approval of the idea.

"How about beers all around?" Uncle Vic suggested. "We can move on to the hard stuff later?"

"Honey," Simon said, "I always end my night with a hard one."

"Yeah," Felix replied, "if he can find some other guy who can get it up."

More cackling. Denny laughed at the men and their feisty friendship.

"Uh," I said, "nine beers it is."

As I made my way towards the troughs, my path took me right by Uncle Harry, and he reached out to grab my arm gently. When I looked at him, he was gesturing for me to lean down.

"Yeah?" I asked as I bent to listen.

"After you get us a drink, would you mind helping Denny?" He requested. "I hate to have him doing all of the work. Felix will use it as leverage next time he throws a party."

"Okay. Sure," I said.

"Then will you talk to Kristal?" He saw my confusion. "The caterer? Ask her if they brought any folding chairs, would you? I have a feeling we'll need them."

I looked around at the group of nine men, Denny, and Bird.

"I think we'll have enough, Harry." I laughed.

"Oh, honey." He patted my forearm as I straightened up. "Wait until the sun starts to set. There'll be queers coming out of the woodwork."

"I'll take your word for it," I said.

Harry swatted at me as I headed towards the troughs to collect beers and the elders continued cackling and roasting each other.

Inside the troughs filled with ice, I found that the beer of choice for the party was the old Iowan staple. Pabst Blue Ribbon. A quick glance at the other troughs let me know there were light beers available—this was a party for queers after all—and there were wine coolers and other fruity drinks in another. Another trough held bottles of water and sodas of different varieties. I wasn't sure where the "hard stuff" was being kept, but I assumed that bottles of liquor and mixers were being set out in the kitchen or tucked away in the cabinets by the catering staff. Having a table full of bottles at a party, sitting out in the hot sun, is just a bad idea. Especially when you have drunk people dancing around, likely to bump into things and send them toppling to the ground.

Somehow, I managed to dig out nine cans of Pabst— or "PBR" as they say in Iowa—and cradled them in my arms so that I could make one trip to the troughs for the elders. When I returned to their semi-circle of cattiness, they were all deeply involved in a discussion about the newest, hottest guys in Hollywood. All of the names being thrown around belonged to men much too young for any of the elder gays, but they were having harmless fun, so I didn't feel the need to remind any of them of the fact. I passed out cans of beers, getting a quick "thank you" from each man before they returned their attention to the conversation at hand.

Once the beers were passed around, and I was certain that the elders would be content for a few minutes with their lawn chairs, beers, and conversation, I headed towards the garage. I slipped my phone out of my pocket to check the time, and it was just a little after seven o'clock. No other guests had arrived yet, or if they had, they were in the house bothering the catering staff. My heart sunk a little as I slid my phone back into my pocket. If no one showed up for the last hurrah for the bar, Harry and Vic would be absolutely heartbroken.

Having their nearest, dearest, and oldest friends over made them happy, but having the younger gays that had seen the invitation at the bar show up would make the party even more memorable for them. It would remind them that their bar and their decades of service to the community actually meant something to the next generation of queers coming up in the world. To be completely blown off by the younger people of the community would be devastating—even if they said nothing about it. I found myself hoping that Uncle Harry was right about more people showing up to the party. Queers coming out of the woodwork would absolutely make my uncles' night.

Inside the garage, it had to be at least ten degrees hotter. The dark, musty interior looked as though it would be a cool respite from the mid-evening sun, but it was the exact opposite. As I stepped through the doorway, I found myself once again wondering if I hadn't chosen the wrong clothes for the party. Denny was on the other side of the garage, partially obscured by my uncles' Lincoln SUV, pulling lawn chairs down from the pegs and racks they were organized on along the massive wall. Before I bothered going to help, I stopped and rolled up the sleeves of my shirt, hoping it would help keep me a little bit cooler.

"Hey," I said as I approached, "Harry thought you could use some help, Denny."

"Harry was right." Denny looked over his shoulder to smile at me.

"Then I'm here to help."

"By the way, my real name is Dennis," He said. "Russy."

"Yeah, I kinda figured. Russell. That's me."

"Uncles." Denny rolled his eyes comically, which I almost didn't catch in the dark. "I've been 'Denny' for as long as I can remember. No one calls me Dennis anymore. Except my mom and dad. But 'Denny' has grown on me, so I actually prefer it."

"Most everyone calls me Russ," I said. "Except my uncles and the elders. I prefer 'Russ,' but 'Russy' doesn't ruin my day or anything, I guess."

"You call them 'the elders' a lot," Denny said, turning back to the wall of chairs. "Why's that? Is that one of their group names I've never heard of before?"

"It's a nicer phrase to use when addressing them rather than 'hey, you old bastards,' I guess?"

Denny laughed uproariously, nearly sending folding chairs falling from their nesting spots to the floor. I reached out and braced them as Denny's laughter sputtered off. When he finally was able to control himself, he turned to look at me, a grin on his face.

"You're funny."

"Thanks," I said simply.

"I still can't believe we never met before today," He said as he pulled another chair down off of a peg. "Boats passing in the night."

"Ships," I said as I took a chair from him and hooked it under my arm.

"What?"

"Ships that pass in the night, and speak each other in passing," I recited as I reached up to grab another chair, "only a signal shown, and a distant voice in the darkness; So on the ocean of life, we pass and speak one another, only a look and a voice, then darkness again and silence."

After I had hooked the second chair under my arm, my eyes caught Denny's, and he was staring at me thoughtfully. Maybe a bit confused?

"Longfellow." I shrugged.

"Oh."

"I'm a writer."

"With a hell of a memory." He quipped. "That's remarkable."

"Remarkable," I said as I reached for another chair, "is writing a poem like *The Theologian's Tale*. I'm unremarkable. Especially as a writer. But it's what I do."

"The doing is what makes you remarkable," Denny said. "Most people don't do what they really love."

"Oh?" I teased. "Then I should be on a white sand beach with a pina colada while chiseled guys in speedos play volleyball in slow motion in front of me, I suppose."

Denny laughed. "Well, it's good work if you can find it, I guess."

"If there's ever an opening, I'll be the first to apply."

"Your uncles have a lot of lawn chairs for two old men who live alone," Denny said. "Well, alone together."

"Now they have me," I said. "The third wheel."

"Wouldn't it be 'fifth wheel?' Cars have four."

"Trikes have three."

"Then you complete the set," Denny said, grabbing another chair, "Unless you're talking about a car. They have four. But a fifth wheel really won't throw off it off-kilter."

"Depends on the quality and placement of the tire."

"If we're stuck on using 'third' in the analogy, why not third nipple? Or third eye? Third testicle?" He asked.

"More to play with in some cases." I smiled to myself.

Denny was laughing again.

Once we both had five of the light folding chairs under each of our arms, twenty between the two of us, we scooted out of the garage carefully. We didn't want to ding Harry's and Vic's Lincoln, and we didn't want to chip the paint in the garage doorframe, after all. The elders cheered when they saw us arriving with all of the chairs. Obviously, they were well into starting their evening buzz, getting ready for the party that hadn't quite started yet.

"Just lean them against the house there!" Uncle Vic shouted when he saw us coming towards them. "People can help themselves if they want a seat. Let's not get too fussy, boys."

"We have Si for that." Felix quipped.

"Stick a dick in it, you old hag." Simon burped.

"Gladly," Felix said before taking a swig of his beer.

Denny and I ignored the elders and went about leaning stacks of chairs against the side of the house, once again being careful to not ding anything in the process. Uncle Harry and Uncle Vic might be forgiving, but a bunch of catty gay men watching meant that any mistake was the opportunity for ridicule, even if it was meant in good fun. I didn't know how Denny would deal with being teased so viciously by the elders, but it wasn't something I enjoyed immensely.

"They're all going to be absolutely impossible to deal with by the end of the night," Denny remarked once we had the chairs in place.

"Yeah," I said. "Once they're loaded, and the sun goes down, it'll be bedlam."

"I can't wait." He rubbed his hands together evilly. "It will be delicious."

"I suppose."

"*Bird!*" Felix shouted from across the yard. "*It's not a real party until we have music. Play something good for us old queers!*"

"You got it!" Bird shouted from the DJ booth.

I looked over to see that he had headphones slipped on, one over his ear, and the other pushed back to leave the other free to hear. The visual completed the whole "DJ aesthetic." We all waited for a few moments as Bird did…whatever it was he did on his laptop to make the music play…and then *Boogie Shoes* by K.C. and the Sunshine Band started to pour from the speakers. I jumped at the sudden noise, especially since it was accompanied by cheers from the elders.

Denny laughed as Uncle Vic and Uncle Harry rose from their chairs to waddle over to the Bluestone patio. Both men kept their beers in hand as they began to, well, *boogie*, bumping hips and shuffling their feet around, not a care in the world. Soon, Felix and Simon—obviously having resolved their feud for a few moments—joined Harry and Vic on the patio to, again, *boogie*. Denny fist pumped for the men and hollered out encouragement as the four older men tore a rug across the massive patio. I couldn't help but smile at seeing my uncles act so young, dancing around their patio, smiling and happy as could be.

"So," Denny turned to me, "I said I'd save a dance for you. Wanna claim it now?"

He held a hand out to me.

"Nah." I waved him off. "Make one of the elders' day and let them dance with a young guy."

"Hey," Denny's smile wilted a bit, "God didn't give us boogie shoes to not use them."

"Well, he gave chickens wings, and they can't even fly."

"But they make excellent appetizers." Denny's smile returned. "Silver linings, Russ."

"Yeah," I said, "but you have to kill the chicken. They probably don't see that as a silver lining."

Denny just stared at me.

"Go on." I waved him off. "Phil looks like he wants a dancing partner."

Denny glanced over at what remained of the semi-circle of elders, a frown slowly blooming on his face, which he tried to mask by forcing a smile back to his lips. After a moment, he retracted his hand and stepped away. I watched him as he traversed the yard and offered his hand to Phil. I couldn't help but smile at the delighted way that Phil snatched at the extended hand and hauled himself out of his lawn chair. Phil passed his beer to Frank and let Denny lead him over to the patio to dance with the others. So, I popped open a lawn chair and sat down by the edge of the house where Denny had left me, and watched everyone utilize their boogie shoes.

Chapter 5
The Littleburg Lesbians

———————————————

"Put your dicks away, you old queens! Us fucking ladies don't want to see that shit!"

Boogie Shoes had just ended, and Bird had started to play some dance song that I'd sounded unfamiliar but was obviously more recently released than something K.C. and the Sunshine Band had recorded. We all jumped at the sound of the growling voice that had emanated from the back door. Harry and Vic turned to see who had announced their presence in such a way, and I rose from my chair for a clear view of the back door. Harry seemed to deflate, and Vic practically squealed and clapped his hands together as the person whom the voice belonged to made themselves known.

Bethany Babington—no shit, that was her real name—chef and owner of Babington's Café, stood at the back door, her hands held aloft grandly to announce her presence. Behind her, bottlenecked in the doorway, was a gaggle of other women, ranging in age from senior—like Bethany—to mid-20s. A smile crept to my face at the sight of Bethany. She was loud, brash, just as quick-witted and salty as the elders, but always kind to me. Thick as a tree trunk, and just as sturdy,

Bethany sported a bowl cut and wore no-nonsense clothes and shoes—even to a party. She was also unbelievably filthy-mouthed because it unnerved the elders to hear a woman say filthy things to them. She'd never met an F-word she couldn't work into conversation. Bethany was my kind of lady.

"Oh, lord," Harry grumbled, barely loud enough to be heard over the song. "Look, Vic. It's the Aged Lesbians. I thought I smelled old shoe leather and men's cologne."

Bethany stepped out of the doorway, her arms lowering to rest at her sides, and a flood of women—about a dozen in all—poured out around her. Some headed directly to the drink troughs, others headed towards the side of the house to fetch lawn chairs, and others just wandered off aimlessly in search of a conversation partner.

The lesbians are such an efficient bunch, I thought to myself.

"Oh, look," Bethany said, "it's Hairy Mary. How are you, you crusty old whore?"

Harry's hands went to his hips, and his head started to jiggle upon his neck rapidly—though I wasn't sure if it was the Parkinson's or rage—but Bethany ignored him and stomped over to accept Vic's outstretched arms. Uncle Vic and Bethany gave each other back-slapping hugs that could probably be heard in the next county as Harry glared at Bethany. When the hug was finally over, Bethany turned to Harry, a bored expression on her face.

"I don't see any food, Mary," She said. "Still as cheap as you were when you carved those personal ads in the cave wall or what?"

"You get older every time I see you, Bethany," Harry said. "Oil of Olay is just spackle for you at this point, isn't it? Wait. Did you get that joke? Do you understand beauty products? I assume you know what spackle is."

"Don't get mad at me because you lost your apartment key," Bethany said as she turned to Vic. "Hairy Mary here thought he was gonna get a visit in the middle of the night from some trick, but Benjamin Franklin just wanted to fly a kite."

"Did you have to bring every damned lesbian in Littleburg with you?" Harry spat.

"Sorry to ruin your sausage fest." Bethany quipped. "But you've been on a diet since Vic locked you down back before color T.V. anyway. Where's Russy?"

Harry's face turned red, and his fists dug into his hips. Before he could volley back some insult about being old, I sprang into motion. Bethany's eyes landed on me as I approached, and she lit up, bouncing in place and throwing her arms out to pull me into a hug. Uncle Vic patted me on the back as Bethany and I hugged ferociously. I hadn't seen the woman in several years, not since I had stayed a week with my uncles the summer before college started.

"Oh, sugar," Bethany cooed, "I haven't seen you in so long! Then I heard you'd be here tonight, and I could barely contain myself."

"Hi, Bethany," I said.

"I hear you're staying with us for a while this time," Bethany pulled back to look me over, her hands still on my arms.

"Vic and me." Harry snapped. "Not *us*. You are not part of this family."

Bethany ignored him, but I shot him a smile to placate him.

"How long will we get you this time?" She asked.

"Undetermined." I shrugged.

"Well," She said, "I'm glad we have you for however long we do."

"Vic and me," Harry said again, "not *us* or *we*."

"Oh, loosen your bra straps." Bethany rolled her eyes as her hands slid from my arms. "Where's the food, Mary? Some stranger answered the door and you have a house full of people in uniforms, but all I see are some drinks and a bunch of busted lawn chairs."

"*Busted?*" Harry hissed.

Before I knew what was happening, Harry and Bethany had launched in on each other, barely inches apart as they traded barbs and cursed each other from one end to the next.

With a sigh, Vic reached over and grabbed ahold of my arm, pulling me close.

"Russ," He said, "why don't you go in and tell them to bring some food out for us? The last thing we need is these two at each other's throats all night."

"They do look hangry," I said.

Vic chuckled and nudged me towards the back door.

"Hurry." He teased.

"Will do."

As quickly as I could without looking improper, I dashed across the patio towards the back door, hoping the caterer had trays of anything they could bring outside. Maybe if Harry and Bethany had something to chow down on and distract themselves with, they wouldn't fight as much. Or at least not as viciously. No sooner had I swung open the back door and stepped inside than Denny had slipped into the house behind me. A glance over my shoulder showed that he was smiling like a dimwitted lost puppy—an adorable, dimwitted lost puppy, but still.

Whether it was my intention or not, I shot him an annoyed look over my shoulder as he closed the door behind us. My hope was that he just happened to be venturing into the house at the same time in order to use the bathroom, but he followed me the few steps down the hallway and into the kitchen. He was hot on my heels as I stepped into the room in search of the caterer. I was prepared to deliver the message from Harry to everyone, but inside I found that the staff was already loading up and gathering trays of food to take outside.

The catering business owner, who I suddenly remembered was named "Kristal" was barking orders like a drill sergeant—but in a slightly more affable manner—as her staff went about doing their jobs expertly. Trays of hamburger sliders, plastic serving cups of potato salad and macaroni salad, small plates of French fries, individual bowls with meatballs in a sweet sauce, spring rolls, enormous trays of watermelon, pineapple, and other fruits, a tray of miniature tacos— everything made my stomach grumble, demanding that I partake in a little bit of everything once I had the chance.

I stood there and listened to Kristal give instructions, Denny at my side, looking around in wonder at everything. Two staff members were each assigned long folding tables— that had appeared from somewhere—and were being told to set them up on the gazebo. The rest of the staff would arrange the food "thoughtfully and beautifully" upon them, and then the party guests could help themselves to the food. That announcement made me take notice of the staff member who had a pile of extra plates cradled in her arms, as well as the utensils guests would need.

Kristal and I exchanged glances and nods as the catering staff filed out of the room like the world's most organized marching band. Obviously, there was nothing I had to discuss with her. She knew her business and how to get things done. Vic had sent me inside for no reason—unless he wanted me out of earshot when Harry and Bethany really laid into each other. It was likely he didn't want me outdoors, taking sides if the two of them got exceptionally ugly with each other. Either way, I was happy to be away from the party. I had some time to myself, away from others, or I would have, if Denny wasn't standing beside me.

Instead of addressing the elephant in the room and asking Denny what in the hell he wanted, I made my way out of the kitchen once again. Heading outside wasn't on my mind, though. The wall of pictures in the hallway was my destination. Denny didn't take the hint and head back outside, but rather, followed me and stood beside me as I looked at the shrine my uncles had created to their life.

I'm the only guy here his age besides Bird, and he talks to him all day long, I'm sure. I thought to myself as I stared up at the framed pictures. *Be nice, Russ.*

"What's all this?" He asked.

"Uh, pictures? The kind they had before smartphones?"

He laughed.

"Harry and Vic did a pretty good job of cataloging their life together," I said. "A long time ago, I remember there just being a few frames on the table in the entryway there. Now, they have this."

"It's impressive."

"Yeah."

"Look," Denny said, "is that you?"

I turned my head to find the picture he had jabbed a finger towards.

"Uh, yeah," I said, taking in the photo, "that's Harry, Vic, my parents, and me. The Gateway Arch in St. Louis."

"Little Russy," He said. "So cute."

"That was kind of our family vacations," I ignored the comment. "At least when my parents were with us. Some tourist-y, educational destination. If it had just been Harry, Vic, and me, it would be Disney World or something. Like that picture over there."

My finger automatically found the picture of Harry, Vic, and me on vacation in Florida. Denny stepped away so that he could get a better look at the photo. I didn't have to join him because I knew the photo well. The three of us were huddled together in front of Cinderella's castle, Mickey Mouse ears on all of our heads. I smiled to myself as I thought of the trip my uncles had taken me on. Even though Florida decided we needed rain during our visit, it was the most glorious three days of my life up until that point.

"You're really close with them, huh?" He said.

"Yeah," I said, "I mean, they've always been big fixtures in my life. When I was young, I was kind of the child they never had. Then, when I told them I was gay, well, the only time I saw them prouder was when I got accepted into college."

Denny chuckled.

"Felix never really took me on many vacations," He said. "My parents weren't as…permissive, I guess?"

"What do you mean?"

"I think Felix is kind of a sore spot in our family history." He explained. "The first openly gay man—and a pretty effeminate one at that. There's still kind of a prejudice and stigma in my family about that. They were never what I'd call supportive of him."

"Is that why you're pretty masculine?" I asked. "So you don't have to worry about your family being supportive?"

"Are you calling me manly?" He turned his head from the photo to grin at me.

"Well, I," I murmured, "I just…you definitely don't take after Felix, I guess?"

Denny appraised me.

"I can definitely see Vic in you more now," He said. "But, there's still that Harry twinkle waiting to come out."

"Thanks," I said. "I guess."

"Where are your parents?" Denny asked.

"New Orleans," I said. "Dad got transferred down there a few years ago with his job. They seemed to really love it down there, so I think they might stay until he retires. We kind of bounced around a lot when I was growing up, I guess? Never went to the same school from one year to the next. But we always had time to visit Harry and Vic."

"Is that why you're kind of taciturn?" Denny asked. "Never had many real friends, so you just kind of insulate yourself?"

For some reason, this amateur attempt to psychoanalyze me hit me wrong.

"I mean, you asked about me being masculine, so I thought—"

"You don't know anything about me." The words escaped my mouth before I had a chance to stop them.

"I've obviously offended you," Denny said, "I just meant—"

"There you two are!" Bethany's voice rang out from the kitchen doorway. "Harry and Felix were wondering where you two were. Food's ready!"

Denny gave me a quick glance and stepped away, heading for the back door.

"Thanks, Bethany," He said quietly as he stepped away.

"You're welcome, honey." She gave him a pat on the shoulder as he slipped by her.

I grimaced, thinking about how rude I had unintentionally been, then turned my attention back to the photos on the wall before me. Just as Denny had, Bethany stepped over to join me at the wall of photos. Unlike Denny, she enjoyed the activity in silence for a few moments, smiling at the photos as her eyes moved from one to another. For several moments, the two of us stood there, gazing up at the photos, reliving memories, enjoying memories that weren't our own, taking in the happiness my uncles had enjoyed throughout their life together.

"Did I ever tell you about the time Hairy Mary and I met?" Bethany asked suddenly.

"Why are you so mean to him?" I chuckled.

"Oh, he loves it," Bethany nudged me with her elbow, a mischievous grin on her face, "so don't let him tell you differently."

"You do seem to bring out his energy."

Bethany laughed. "I was working in the cafeteria at the elementary school? Talk about underappreciated work."

"I can imagine."

"I was down at the grocery store, minding my own business, picking up a few things for home," She said, "I was married then. *To a man.*"

A hand went to my chest, and I opened my mouth in feigned shock.

"I know, right?" She cackled. "This ole lesbian was once married to an honest to goodness man."

"Don't tell the other lesbians," I whispered. "They'll take away your plaid shirts."

"They wouldn't dare!" She said. "Well, I was down the produce aisle and met an interesting gentleman."

"Harry?"

"No," She said. "Morty."

She jabbed her thumb towards a picture of Morty with my uncles.

"He had me pegged immediately," Bethany said, "He knew that I was born a dyke and would always be a dyke."

"Bethany…"

"I'll say what I want, damnit. I've been through enough to have the privilege." She glowered at me for a second. "Anyhow, maybe I was looking at the melons too long or something, but something told him we were kindred. Well, in the queer way, I guess. He didn't say anything about his suspicions then, though. We got to talking, he found out I worked in the cafeteria, and he asked if I'd ever been to something called *A Straight Line*. Of course, then I didn't even want to accept feelings I'd had about other women. I was happy to push those down. So, I'd never been to the bar before. Actually, I'd never been to *any* bar. I was a *good little wife* then."

"I just can't picture it." I laughed.

"Well," She continued, "Morty said they were thinking about starting to serve some food, help get more business, you know, so he asked if I would be interested in applying for the job as their cook."

"You cooked at *A Straight Line?*"

"Well, for the first few years they served food," She said. "Listen to the story, damnit. I'm getting there. Well, once I found out what your uncles' bar was all about, I was scared to go. I was scared to tell my husband that the *queer bar* in town wanted me to apply for a job. I was scared at how excited it all made me."

"That's awful."

"Yeah," She sighed, "but, the cafeteria didn't pay shit. And I was tired of always being the *good little wife,* always depending on a man to make sure things were taken care of. So, I went down to the bar, asked to see Morty. And then I met Bang Bang."

"Oh my." I teased.

"'*Oh my'* is right." She laughed. "I'd never seen such in my life up until that moment. *A man in a dress?* But Bang Bang took me to Harry—who wasn't so happy to see me—but he gave me the job on the spot at Bang Bang's request. For the first two years that the bar served food, I was the one cooking and plating it. All by myself. Before it became too big of an operation to do on my own. So, they brought in more staff. Over those few years, I saved up money, got rid of my husband, found Georgina, and decided that I could run my own restaurant."

I just stared at her.

"Because of Hairy Mary, I'm a proud old dyke with my own business and wonderful memories of the life I shared with Georgina before her passing. I needed a little queer magic to set me on the right path to the right career and into the arms of the love of my life."

"Sounds like it was more Bang Bang who should get the credit, actually."

"Maybe," Bethany said, "but Hairy Mary didn't have to give me a chance. Bang Bang knew what I needed, he knew what Hairy Mary needed, but all she could do was push us in the right direction. We had to be the ones to reach out and snatch the opportunity. Your uncle may be an old bitch, but he's good people. He's why I am who I am today. But I suppose we can give Bang Bang some of the credit."

Again, she nudged me with her elbow. I chuckled as she winked at me.

"If it weren't for your uncles and their bravery—and *my God, Bang Bang just being who she is*—Littleburg would be an awful place." Bethany sighed. "You should-a seen this place forty years ago. You know, when your uncles opened that bar, it was like Dorothy stepping out of her house from black and white into technicolor. Things just…became more beautiful."

"What a fittingly gay metaphor."

"You can joke all you want, but that's exactly what it was like," She said. "A fog being burnt off by the sun. Finally, we could all see again. That's your uncles, Russy. They made Littleburg a lovely little town for everyone to coexist. Sure, they got knocked down time and time again, but they kept getting up. For them. For us. Even if none of these pictures were on this wall, they've led an exceptional life. An exceptional life of service to their community."

"That's very sweet of you, Bethany."

"Well, I'll give Hairy Mary credit where credit is due." She sighed. "But I'll never stop getting under his skin every chance he gives me."

"I would expect nothing less." I chuckled.

"Why don't you get out there and get you some food, sugar?" She nudged me towards the kitchen. "You're skinnier than the last time I saw you."

"Thanks?"

"Go on." She swatted at me playfully.

Heeding the words of the "aged lesbian," I made my way down the hall and away from the wall of pictures. Bethany turned back to the wall to continue taking in all of the wonderful memories.

"Hey," Bethany's voice stopped me short, "where's Clint? Didn't he come with you?"

With a sigh, I turned to her.

"We don't all find our Georgina, Bethany." I shrugged.

"Oh, Russy," She said. "I'm sorry, sugar."

I waved her off. Bethany looked thoughtful for a moment.

"Your uncles know?"

"Of course," I said. "I had to give them a reason why I wanted to stay here indefinitely without him, right?"

"That grandson of Felix's isn't too bad to look at," She said. "It's been a while since I've been with a man, but I'd definitely call him *hot*. Do you young'uns still use *hot*?"

"Sometimes." I shrugged again.

"Well, then that's what he is," She said. "He'd probably make a good dance partner. Or at least someone to enjoy a plate of food or a drink with at a party."

"Fuck off, Bethany."

She laughed. "Fair enough."

I smiled at her, then she went back to looking at pictures, and I made my way outside where the sun was setting and night was creeping up on us. As if announcing my arrival, the strings of lights that had been hung up suddenly switched on. And I was hit with the realization that the crowd outside had doubled. Apparently, the queers had answered the call.

Either that or they smelled the food. When I saw the group of younger gay men huddled around Uncle Vic and Uncle Harry, a smile came to my face.

Their community hadn't let them down.

Chapter 6
Queer Mythology

Denny was standing by one of the drink troughs, a can of PBR in hand, engaged in conversation with a young woman I didn't recognize. Obviously, she was one of the women who had arrived with Bethany and the "Littleburg Lesbians." He was smiling and carrying on an animated conversation with her, so obviously I hadn't upset him too much with my harsh tone. Giving him a second appraisal, I realized that Bethany wasn't wrong. Denny wasn't bad to look at all. In fact, he *was* hot. The black jeans and t-shirt definitely did his body favors. He seemed pleasant enough, personality-wise. I shook my head to clear my thoughts.

As I surveyed the massive backyard, my smile grew. People were in the gazebo, helping themselves to food. People were standing by the drink troughs, carrying on excitedly about…whatever. The elders were stationed in their chairs, holding court with the younger generation, smiles plastered to their faces due to all of the attention. A large group of people was dancing to *I Wanna Dance with Somebody (Who Loves Me)* by Whitney Houston. And my uncles looked absolutely over-the-moon happy as a group of younger queers fought for their attention. Knowing that people my age, and maybe even younger, were so interested in talking with the older generation warmed my heart.

Maybe tomorrow would be a different, and all of the younger queers would forget all about the wisdom and experience the elders could impart; they'd forget how fun older queers can be. But for this one night that was important to my uncles, they were giving back what my uncles had given them. If that didn't make the whole night worthwhile, I didn't know what would.

I decided to be a grown-up and not be too scared of such a large crowd. Instead of going to my uncles, where I felt safest and most confident, I traversed the yard over to the gazebo. I hadn't had much to eat since lunch, which we'd had fairly early in the day since so much had to be done to get ready for the party, so my stomach was grumbling.

For the last few months, before I decided to bite the bullet and come stay with my uncles, I had been alone. Holed up in my apartment, focusing on deadline after deadline, pretending the world didn't exist, I rarely stepped foot outside of my apartment until after dark. New York may be the city that never sleeps, but at a certain time of day, the crowds waned in my neighborhood. I could go down to the bodega without too much human interaction. I could have food delivered. I didn't need another person in the world to remind me that people don't always turn out to be as great as you make them out to be in your head.

Of course, those months left me distrustful of others, afraid of large crowds, and what Harry called a "general sourpuss." I never said it to him outright, but how is a guy supposed to enjoy being around other people when the person you loved and trusted most proved they didn't deserve your love or trust to begin with? It only makes sense that something like that would make a person need a while to recover before putting themselves out there again. Not that I'd ever been one to just throw myself out there, like Harry, Felix, Simon, or Bang Bang. I definitely wasn't a Bethany. I was just some guy needing to heal a pretty deep wound and enjoy the emotional—if not financial—support of his uncles. In time I'd be normal again.

Right?

Most of the people in the gazebo who were helping themselves to the quickly disappearing food were not familiar to me. Most of them were the younger queers Harry and Vic had invited—who might have been regulars to the bar, but not to me—and they generally didn't notice my arrival. As is common in our community, a few of the guys gave me sideways glances, checking out the new guy in the vicinity. Some even looked pleased with what they saw, much to my delight. But none of them bothered greeting me or tried striking up a conversation. They were focused on the food and whomever else they knew that was along for the trip to the buffet.

That's another thing, a difference between generations of queers. If you walk into a room of elder queers, they tend to get right in your business immediately. *What's your name? I'm so-and-so. What do you do? Are you single? Married? Out/In? Welcome, welcome, welcome to the community.* Younger queers take a more accepting and easier world for granted. They don't feel as much of a need to welcome other queers into the community and find out their stories. I guess, growing up around so many older gay men, it just became normal for me to expect other people in the community to welcome a person with open arms.

I was an old gay man in a young gay man's body.

I had grabbed a plate and was helping myself to a hamburger slider when a voice startled me.

"Oh, Russy!" A man's voice chirped. "Help us out!"

I turned to find Floyd, one of The Flirtatious Five, standing by the tray full of individual servings of potato and macaroni salad, standing with one of the women who had arrived with Bethany and her gaggle.

"Sure, Floyd," I said. "What's up?"

I quickly slid two of the sliders onto my plate.

"Now," Floyd said as I approached, plate in hand, "how long have your uncles been together? I can't remember.

I was telling Sheila that I knew they were pretty young when they met."

"Forty-eight years," I responded, to which Sheila's eyes grew wide.

"We just say fifty." I shrugged. "It's easier to remember."

"Jeeeeeeeeezus." Sheila exhaled. "That's a long time to put up with one person. Joanie and I have been together for three years, and I think about smothering her in her sleep at least once a day."

"That's healthy," Floyd patted her arm. "Totally healthy."

I laughed, though it was forced.

Some of us would love to have someone we want to smother in their sleep.

"I was just telling Sheila about your uncles," Floyd said. "She moved here last year with her partner Joanie—"

"Joan. We just *call* her 'Joanie,'" Sheila said.

"—and," Floyd said, "they've only been to the bar a few times. They never had the opportunity to really meet your uncles."

"They're something." I nodded towards the semi-circle of lawn chairs where my uncles and the others were holding court. "They'd be happy to have you go introduce yourself."

"I'll do that," Sheila said. "It was so nice of them to invite us. Well, Vic did. Harry seemed indifferent."

"He has a thing against lesbians," Floyd murmured.

I laughed. "He really doesn't. He's just putting on a show. He loves all of his queer community. He just has a funny way of showing it."

"Thank goodness," Sheila chuckled. "We're really excited to see Bang Bang perform tonight. We saw her a few weeks ago at *A Straight Line,* and—is she here yet?"

"I haven't seen her." I shrugged.

"I was telling Sheila and Joanie earlier how Bang Bang is the one that started the school supplies drive years and years ago. The Drag Queen Reading Hour at the library. The food pantry over at Gentry's. Bang Bang has altruism running out of every orifice."

Sheila and I both turned up our noses comically. Floyd grinned.

"She's done a lot for the community," I said. "Queer or otherwise. I've been around for a while, but even I don't know all she's done."

"Even when she had nothing, she made sure the people of this community were taken care of, Russ," Floyd said with a firm nod. "Granted, not everyone was happy about it at first."

"What do you mean?" Sheila asked.

"Well, for example, the school supplies drive?" Floyd said. "A lot of the more puritanical parents in this town accused Bang Bang of having *ulterior motives* for helping the children. As though Bang Bang was trying to align the queens with little children to groom them or something. Turns my stomach to remember it. But Bang Bang still took school supply donations, went door to door asking for money, posted flyers…by the beginning of the school year, every kid in this town starting school had the best. And it's been that way ever since. Now, it's gotten easier over the years, now that people are all friendly with Bang Bang and admire her philanthropy, but it wasn't so way back when she started. Even some of the queers in this community told her to give it up."

Floyd raised his voice in admonishment of some of the people around us, and to remind them we all should be more altruistic.

"Bang Bang just did what Bang Bang does," Floyd said. "She wouldn't take 'no' for an answer. And that's why Littleburg has one of the lowest drop-out rates, one of the highest percentages of kids who go off to trade school or college, no one goes hungry, and you'd be hard-pressed to find a single person who can't read. Drag Queen Reading Hour at the library wasn't just for little kids. Bang Bang would stay and help older people in the community learn as well. They were cautious of her at first, but once they realized how dedicated she was to making sure they could read and live their lives with less struggles and more accessibility, they all fell in love with her. She's also why the non-queers and queers of this town get along so well. She's been one hell of an ambassador over the years."

"I can't wait to be formally introduced." Sheila was in awe.

"Well," Floyd said slyly, "the Bang Bang you meet, and the Bang Bang who does charity work are two different people. She's…*standoffish?*"

That's not the Bang Bang I know, I thought to myself.

"She doesn't like people to fuss," Floyd said.

"Even so," Sheila said, "I can't wait."

I had busied myself, stuffing my mouth full of a slider. One, I was getting hungrier by the second, listening patiently to Floyd, and two, I wanted my mouth full so I couldn't correct him about Bang Bang's demeanor. If she was "standoffish" to anyone, it was probably because she didn't want everyone begging her for something all of the time. Besides, she was kind of a regional celebrity. Even queens need their privacy from time to time.

While Frank prattled on about Bang Bang, the community in general, how lovely the party was going, and other such things, the sun fully set around us, leaving us all bathed in the twinkling glow of the lights strung around the yard. I also managed to scarf down a few helpings of potato salad, eat a serving of fries, and inhale a few spring rolls. My tummy thanked me.

Bird was playing a slow song as Frank and Joanie finally drifted away, obviously to find their partners for a dance or to make conversation with someone more inclined to participate in said conversation. As I stood there, realizing that I'd been left alone in the gazebo, an empty plate in my hands, *Power of Two* by Indigo Girls played in the background. The party had swelled to at least a hundred, maybe a hundred-and-fifty, people, and while not everyone was slow dancing with their partner of choice, the dance floor had spilled past the Bluestone patio and out onto the lawn.

Most of the elders were still in their semi-circle of chairs, adoringly watching the other queers dancing happily. Vic and Harry were nowhere in sight, so I assumed that meant they were somewhere amongst the throngs of people dancing away to the lesbian anthem. That was kind of out of character for Harry, dancing to a slow song and all, but it was possible Vic might have convinced him to join him on the dance floor. Watching all of the people in our community enjoying the lovely evening—and the perfectly executed party thrown by my uncles and Kristal—I should have been thrilled. I just felt…empty.

Looking over the crowd of people, how surrounded by members of the community who loved and supported my uncles and their bar—and were sad to see them retiring—was nice. It was more than nice. But it just made me remember how alone I was in the world. The people on the dance floor were holding each other gently or gripping each other tightly, their bodies pressed closely together. It had been months since I'd had someone hold me...at all. I didn't have a partner like my uncles, or Bethany, or any number of the other people who had come to the party. I was just a chronically gloomy, socially awkward gay man who would probably end up all alone for life.

Nothing like a party to flip a guy's mood.

"Hey," I jumped when Denny popped up at my side in the gazebo.

"*Jesus!*" I gasped, but laughed once I realized that I was in no immediate danger.

"Sorry," He said, leaning closer towards me. "You just looked like you were lonely over here. Full, but lonely."

"Uh, yeah." I agreed. "Definitely full."

"What are you doing up here all alone?"

I had to stop myself from telling Denny that I *was* alone. I didn't have a special someone to forcefully drag me out onto the dance floor. But then he'd insist on dancing with me, and I wasn't so sure I wanted to dance with Denny.

"Floyd was telling Sheila and me about Bang Bang and his many philanthropic endeavors over the years," I said. "I was stuffing my face…and I guess everyone wandered off to dance in the meantime. So, here I am."

"Bang Bang is pretty beloved, right?"

"Pretty mythological at this point," I said. "She hasn't even shown her face tonight, and she seems to be all that anyone talks about. Well, besides Harry and Vic, I guess."

"Well, you know," Denny produced a beer from his pocket and held it out to me, "what they say about our community?"

"No?" I accepted the beer with a smile.

"Everywhere we go, we sprinkle magic," He said with a smile, producing a second beer, seemingly out of thin air, for himself.

We both popped our tops and tapped our cans together. The first sip of the beer hit just right, proving to be something I needed desperately but hadn't been aware of. Of course, when you're feeling maudlin and socially anxious at a party, a beer always helps.

"They say a lot of things about our community," I said.

"Such as?" He grinned.

"Well," I said, "depends on who's saying it, I guess. It could be good or bad."

"Let's talk about the good then."

"Well," I thought about it, "we're well-groomed. Well-spoken. We care about personal hygiene. Fashion."

"We're good cooks."

"We have a ton of disposable income," I added.

"We throw fabulous parties, obviously," He said as he waved out over the crowd.

"Excellent taste in music, too."

"Obviously," He said. "We queers know good music."

"We're incredibly funny and clever."

"We are good with a quip."

I took a giant slug of my beer.

"Though, here we are, drinking brewskies like a couple of wallflowers while everyone else dances," Denny said. "I think that might prove that we're not as fabulous as everyone thinks."

"Maybe."

"I haven't seen one single bit of debauchery tonight, though," Denny added. "So, that disproves another myth."

"Which myth?" I asked, then finished my beer.

"That we're all sex-crazed maniacs who will sleep with anyone who comes along," Denny said. "The world would have you believe that this party was just one big bacchanalia. An orgy of epic proportions. Genitalia flying."

"Oh?"

"That's what a lot of the world thinks of us queers," He said. "It's all about sex, sex, sex with us, ya' know?"

"Yeah. I guess so."

"It's just what we do. Sex, sex, sex."

I looked over at him just as he tipped his beer back and guzzled the rest. I had only seen Denny drink one other beer before the ones we had just shared. He lowered the beer, wiped his mouth with the back of his hand, then belched as quietly as possible.

"You drunk?" I asked.

"On these?" He looked down at the can. "Absolutely not. But they're not making me any less social, I guess."

"Gotcha."

"You drunk?"

"On one beer?" I chuckled.

"Fair enough." He smiled.

We stared at each other for several moments, both of us seemingly unsure of where else we could take such a conversation. Then I had an idea.

"Wanna exchange blowjobs in the garage?" I asked.

"Thought you'd never ask." He smiled.

A Straight Line

Chapter 7
Thump-a-Thump & Fireworks

"So, that," Denny's head thumped against the wall of the garage, "was, uh, *oof*, when we decided it was best to, *uhnf*, split up, I guess."

Thump-a-thump.

The dance music that was playing outside thumped along.

Thump-a-thump.

My head was bobbing up and down, Denny's fingers were trailing through my hair, and he hadn't stopped talking since I had dropped to my knees in the dark garage and took him in my mouth. It wasn't unpleasant, I guess, having someone tell me why they were single while I sucked them off, but it was unusual. I'd never had a guy try to get to know me while I was giving him a blowjob. Then again, I'd never offered to exchange sexual favors with a guy at a party after having known him for a few hours. However, between the quick adrenaline the beer provided, the music, the dancing, the merriment of the gays, and the deep well of loneliness in my gut, doing something so out of character had seemed like a great idea in the moment.

In the few minutes I had been kneeling before him, Denny had managed to encapsulate why he was single and how his last relationship had fallen apart. I also knew how he had come to live with Bird—old college roommate helps out a newly single, practically homeless friend—and why he chose to come back to Littleburg of all places. I tried to listen to the background information he gave me on himself, but I was kind of busy with… *other things.* I didn't know if it was ruder to ignore what he was saying or to perform a less than satisfactory blowjob. No one had ever given me advice on what to do in such an odd situation. It was altogether ignored in the Gay 101 course.

"So—*oh god*," Denny groaned, "I guess you could—*oh, just like that*—could say I've been single ever since. It's not so bad, it's—*shit, that's amazing*—but I get lonely sometimes."

I tried not to roll my eyes up at him as he carried on, and I bobbed up and down on him.

"Bird keeps me from getting too lonely, I guess, but— *I'm getting close, fuck*—but he's not loquacious or anything," Denny said. "Mostly—*oh shit*—he just makes enough noise so that the house isn't too quiet, and—*fuuuuuuuuck.*"

Being familiar with the sounds Denny was making, I sped up my movements, my head bobbing up and down faster, wanting him to finish. At least when it was my turn, his mouth would be too busy to tell me about what he'd had for breakfast or what he wanted to be when he grew up. Or about some cute squirrel he'd seen at the park. Something about Denny, though, told me that he probably talked in his sleep. He probably talked while brushing his teeth. He. Was. A. Talker.

"It's great not being, *uhnf*, alone," Denny said. "*Holy shit.* I love not being alone. *Here it comes.*"

Then he was spilling forth, and his words became a garble of sounds and groans. Which was fine with me. At least he wasn't trying to teach me more about himself while he orgasmed, and I swallowed. For a few moments, after his orgasm had subsided, Denny stroked my head and ran his fingers through my hair while I nursed him. Then he was pulling me up off of my knees and dragged me close to him. I knew his intentions and wanted to avoid that if at all possible. So, instead of meeting his lips with my own, I gave him a sly smile and shoved him downwards.

With Denny silent—for obvious reasons—I was able to concentrate on the goal I had set out for myself when I had so brazenly propositioned him in the gazebo. *I just wanted to feel something.* With the thump-a-thump of the music outside, the voices of party attendees having the time of their lives, and Denny on his knees in front of me, I did feel something. Denny was doing a more than adequate job of the task that had been assigned to him, so it felt nice. I hadn't had another guy touch me in a sexual way in months—mostly of my own choosing. But I mostly felt lonelier.

How can I feel so lonely with a party going on yards away and a guy giving me head?

Has a time come when getting a blowjob from a virtual stranger doesn't perk me up?

Not that I was in the habit of doing such things, but going completely against character was something I thought would help snap me out of my mood. At least a little bit. I didn't think that propositioning Denny would completely change my life or even fix every single problem I had, but I thought it would at least make me happier for a few moments. And I guess I was a little happy. What guy *isn't* happy getting head, right? But knowing that Denny was just a stranger at a party—admittedly, a nice, fun, talkative one—and not someone I was in a relationship with just reminded me that I was alone. The guy with the most intimate part of me in this mouth was just some guy.

It hadn't been at the forefront of my mind when I had woken up earlier in the day—trading blowjobs in a dark garage with a stranger while the party raged on outside. Of course, I hadn't even known that Denny existed until he arrived at the party, so how could it have been a thought? I braced my hand against one of the studs in the garage wall behind me as the other hand went to the back of Denny's head. He was hungrily going to town, obviously immersed in and laser-focused on the activity that had been my suggestion. He was doing a pretty good job, so he hadn't lied about not being drunk when I had asked. The reason I had asked was to make sure he wouldn't say "yes" as a simple bad drunken decision while feeling euphoric at a party and then regret it later.

Non-inebriated consent is the best consent.

It's the only consent that counts, actually.

I could feel myself building towards orgasm as I looked down through the darkness of the garage to the dark blur that was the top of Denny's head. I didn't want to admit it, but even with my dour mood—which usually kills my sex drive—Denny was bringing me to the brink. The guy obviously knew what was he was doing. For the briefest, and most blissful of moments, I forgot all about being alone, feeling like I'd be alone forever, being a sourpuss, being socially awkward, and just gave myself over to the feelings lower in my body. As soon as I did that, my body went rigid, and stars exploded in my eyes as my other hand grabbed at Denny's head. He continued to forcefully bob up and down on me as I rode the waves of my orgasm and emptied myself into his mouth.

Then it was over.

Luckily, my mood only went halfway back to sour.

Ecstasy made it impossible to be downright grumpy.

"*Jesus,*" I muttered as Denny released me and rose to stand in front of me, a massive grin on his face.

"I think you enjoyed that." He chuckled.

I reached up and put a hand over his mouth as I leaned my head back against the garage wall.

"*Shhhhhhut up.*" I chuckled hoarsely. "Don't ruin this."

Denny was obedient, letting me hold a hand over his mouth as the last bit of the euphoria drained from my body. I was left sagging against the garage wall, feeling as though some tension I hadn't known I'd been carrying around with me was drained away. Metaphorically speaking, of course. Slowly, I let my hand fall from his mouth. My palm was a little wet with his spit, and, well, possibly other fluids, which was kind of gross, but easily fixed. I let my hand fall to my side, making a mental note to find some soap and water before I did anything else.

"I know I talk too much," He said. "It's a nervous thing, I think."

"You don't like crowds, either?" I managed to mumble, my eyes closed.

"No," He said. "I'm not great around cute guys."

"Well," I said, tilting my head to look at him in the darkness, "you're in luck. There aren't any here. I mean, besides you, obviously."

He sighed.

"You don't think much of yourself, do you?"

"I just let a stranger blow me in my uncles' garage," I said. "After I blew him. It's a redundant question."

"I'm not a stranger." Denny turned to lean back against the garage wall next to me. "We've known each other several hours now. Shared a beer. Our uncles are friends."

"Okay," I said. "Fine. We're not exactly *strangers*."

"And you should think more of yourself."

"Look, Denny," I said as I turned my head to look at him, "you seem like a nice guy. Especially after what you, uh, just did, but—"

"You're welcome. And thank you." He grinned.

"—*thank you*—but you don't know me," I said. "I mean, isn't it a little early in the relationship to start psychoanalyzing each other?"

"I do that, too." He sighed. "Cute guys. Awkward. I don't know when to shut up sometimes."

"I don't hate it," I said, reaching down to tuck myself away and zip up my pants—an action Denny mirrored. "But I just—I've kind of been in a mood for a few months."

"That's cool," He said, wiping his hands against his pants once he was zipped up. "I mean, I get it. You don't want to talk about it, but obviously, you went through a break-up, too, right?"

"Yeah."

"So, we don't have to talk about it," He said. "But…maybe you could enjoy the company of a *not really a stranger* for one night? I don't really know anyone here besides Bird, you, and the elders. And, I mean, after the blowjobs, what's a night of hanging out?"

I laughed.

"Am I asking too much?"

"No," I said. "That's fairly reasonable, I guess. I just— don't expect much. I'm kind of committed to this 'woe is me' mood right now. It's kind of my thing. Okay?"

"I can work with that," He said.

"Good," I said, pushing away from the wall.

"But," He said, grabbing ahold of my arm so that I was forced to turn and look at him, "you won't be such a sourpuss by the end of the night."

I stared at him briefly; the music that had been thumping away outside, suddenly stopped.

"We'll see." I frowned, wondering why the music had stopped.

"Is it too much to ask for a kiss after that?" He asked quietly.

"No kissing," I said. "No dancing. But I'll try to be a decent party date otherwise."

"Okay."

"And keep this between us," I said. "Please?"

"Sure."

"You're upset now."

"No," He said, and his tone suggested he was being genuine. "Just trying to work on the 'talking too much' thing to prove to you that I can improve."

I started to laugh, but then loud banging noises, almost like gunshots, sounded from outside. Denny and I both jumped, nearly coming out of our skin as our eyes grew wide. Racing for the door was obviously a shared plan because we both nearly collided as we ran for it, both grabbing for the knob at the same time. I yanked my hand away so that Denny could open it for us, then we both spilled out into the backyard.

What the fuck is going on?

Is everyone okay?

My mind was racing with macabre ideas of what could have possibly made the gunshot noises as we left the garage and shut the door behind us. As soon as we turned away from the garage, I looked out towards the Bluestone patio and the rest of the yard where the party attendees would be. Every color of the rainbow seemed to light up the sky around us. All of the party attendees had their backs to us, their heads raised skyward. Denny and I both looked up to see fireworks bursting in the sky above us. *Ooooooh's* and *aaaaaah's* and hoots emanated from everyone at the party as fireworks in every color of the rainbow exploded in the sky above us.

Denny nudged me, and I looked over to see him smiling brilliantly and gesturing up at the fireworks. I allowed myself to give him a smile back, then began scanning the crowd for my uncles. Just as I had expected, I found them both standing by their chairs in the semi-circle, their backs to me as they held hands and looked up at the sky. Felix was near them, so I gestured for Denny to follow me. The two of us made our way through the crowd, pushing past people as politely as possible, and finally made our way over to Harry and Vic.

As soon as I reached my uncles, and I laid a hand on Harry's shoulder, he started as though he was about to come out of his skin. I had to hide a grin at startling him in such a way so easily. He turned to see who had grabbed him, and the smile on his face at seeing the fireworks grew even more. Harry held a finger up to me and reached into his pocket, pulling out his phone. The "pops" and "bangs" of the fireworks were too loud for him to explain what he wanted me to know, so he just woke his phone and held the screen up for me to read.

The top of the screen said: "*Karen*." Which usually isn't a great thing to see pop up in your text messages. It usually means the cops are going to be called. However, the message proved that this particular Karen was not typical.

Turn off the music and watch the sky. We have a gift from Bang Bang for you.

So, Bang Bang hadn't arrived at the party yet because she was setting up a firework display for my uncles' last hurrah for *A Straight Line*? That was nice, but it didn't make a ton of sense. I couldn't imagine that Bang Bang was off in the distance, giant blowtorch in hand, igniting each firework that was flying high into the sky and bursting in a rainbow of colors. Something else had to be going on with Bang Bang. Also, I kind of wanted to know who Karen was and how she knew my uncles and Bang Bang. When Harry saw the confused look on my face, he smiled.

"*She's a neighbor!*" He managed to scream over the noise of the fireworks.

Then he went back to staring up at the sky and "*ooooohing*" and "*aaaaaahing*" with everyone else at the party. Uncle Vic glanced over his shoulder at me, the joy at what was transpiring above us etched on his face. When he saw my hand on Harry's shoulder, the joy became palpable, and he reached over to put his hand over mine. The three of us stood there, Vic's and my hand on Harry's shoulder as we looked up at the queer magic flying through the sky.

I want to say that I felt my mood improve, that maybe I didn't feel so glum as I had been for so long. Between the fireworks above us, the community gathering around my uncles in one of the most profound moments in their lives, my full belly, and the blowjobs Denny and I had exchanged, I should have been the happiest little gay man in the world. But I just wasn't.

What was wrong with me that I couldn't enjoy one really great evening in the history of my family?

Why couldn't I focus on being happy for my uncles and the fact that they had led extraordinary lives that had obviously touched and meant so much to so many people in the community?

Why couldn't I just enjoy a goddamn fireworks display?

As I stood there listening to every hoot and holler, inspired by the fireworks display, the faces of everyone lighting up in alternating red, blue, green, purple, white, yellow, orange, I tried to figure out what was wrong with me. Millions of people in the world had gone through what I'd gone through in the last few months of my life. A relationship broken beyond repair. A career that wasn't exactly soaring towards the stratosphere. Deciding to move back home—*even if it wasn't technically with their parents*—and trying to figure out what life meant if it wasn't going the way they had expected.

A glance over at Felix let me know that he was having a special moment with Denny as well. Denny had draped his arm over Felix's shoulder, hugging him to his side as they stared up at the sky above. Denny's back was to me, so I let my eyes wander over his body, let my thoughts run wild. *Maybe the garage incident doesn't have to be the only thing we do.* From what I could make out in the flashing lights, there were other enjoyable things Denny's body might be able to offer. Which was stupid to think. He was a *virtual stranger,* and I was just a big sourpuss. Why would I bother with Denny further if I wasn't sure that I was in the right frame of mind to start something new?

Doesn't a guy need more than a few months out of a long-term relationship before he tries to start a new one?

Harry and Vic had gotten a sign that they meant something—to each other, their friends, their family, the community. They had over a hundred people at a party in their backyard simply because they were selling their bar. They had food and drinks and dancing and laughter and stories about all of the good times had over the decades. They had a freaking surprise firework display arranged by their best friend...*just because.*

I desperately needed someone to give me a sign.

To give me a reason to move forward with my life now that I had Harry and Vic to lean on for support while I did so.

I needed...

Which hand was I supposed to wash?

I looked at the hand on Harry's shoulder—the one Vic's hand was draped over—as my mind raced. Then I remembered it was my other hand.

Thank God.

Chapter 8
Where There's a Drag Queen,
There's a Way

"*Russ?*"

I was violently washing my hands in the kitchen sink, and Denny was nearby, picking at the caterer's trays that were laid out on the kitchen island, spotted with leftover food, when the woman approached me. Denny had already given his hands a thorough wash at my suggestion before he picked through the food that was still laid out. Of course, getting sick from using his unwashed hands to eat was unlikely. We hadn't done anything *too* disgusting, but in case other people happened to pick off the tray as well, it was respectful to wash his hands. Besides, good hygiene never killed anyone.

The fireworks display had gone on for several minutes, and all of the attendees—but especially my uncles—were touched by the extravagant show organized by Bang Bang. I was no expert, but I knew such a gift couldn't have been inexpensive. Bang Bang's financial situation wasn't something I was privy to, but I wondered how many drag shows she had performed to pay for such a thing. Then again, knowing Bang Bang's resourcefulness, she had probably gotten people in the community to chip in for the show. Or she had charmed somebody into doing it for free. It wasn't totally outside the realm of possibilities knowing how charming and resourceful Bang Bang could be.

Where the fuck was she?

It was well after dark, more than four hours into the party, and there hadn't been a single indication that Bang Bang was actually showing up in person to the party. Like everyone else, including my uncles, I was under the impression that Bang Bang was going to put on one of her infamous shows right there in the backyard. I'd assumed that the gazebo would be her stage. She'd done worse than perform surrounded by trays of food—though the caterer had already cleared those away and put them in the house. What was left, anyway. From what I remembered, Bang Bang had a way of commanding a stage, microphone or not, so she could have managed. All she had to do was show up.

In fact, I really, *really* needed Bang Bang to show up. Something told me that if I could see her, be in the presence of her effervescence—and bawdy dick jokes—my mood would actually improve. Even if it was only for the length of her show, I would love to forget my troubles and just laugh for a little while. Bang Bang had a way of bringing the sun out on the cloudiest of days. If ever there was going to be a sign that everything would be okay with my life, it would be Bang Bang putting on a special, intimate show just for my uncles' retirement.

My mind flashed through all the memories I had as a child, an adolescent, a teenager, when I'd come to visit my uncles. We had always gone out of our way to catch at least one of Bang Bang's shows while I was in town visiting. After the shows, Bang Bang always took time to see me, catch up on how I was doing, and make me laugh. I hadn't thought about it over the years, but ever since the first time we met, when she offered me candy, she always seemed to have candy on her every other time we ran into each other. Even when I had been visiting at spring break during my last year of high school, Bang Bang just happened to have a candy bar on hand when I came to see her show with Harry and Vic.

After her show that night, she had held court with Harry, Vic, and me at the back of the club in one of the corner booths, telling filthy jokes, having drinks, and laughing uproariously. Of course, I had been underage then, so soda had been my drink of choice at *A Straight Line*—no point in getting my uncles and the bar into trouble. But I hadn't needed to be inebriated to die laughing at Bang Bang's irreverent humor. Bang Bang had made me feel like I was the only person in the world that mattered. Instead of working the room and basking in her regional celebrity status, she had taken a break for the night, especially for me. And, at the end of the night, when the bar was starting to close, and she rose from the booth to give me a hug, she slipped me a giant chocolate bar she had produced out of nowhere. With a wink, she had said:

Even if an evening has been perfect, it can still be improved with chocolate.

I guess it had been her way of saying that things can and will get better—no matter what had happened moments before. For some reason, I had never forgotten that. Maybe that's why, as lonely and downtrodden as I had felt for the last few months, I still held out hope. It was most likely why moving in with Harry and Vic had been my first choice after deciding I had to make a change. I knew that even though my life had gone to shit—hadn't turned out the way I had expected—being around my uncles and my community would somehow make it better. Eventually.

Of course, the next thing that came out of her mouth was:

Unless you can find a hot guy with a big dick. Then tell the chocolate to go fuck itself.

I smiled at the memory as I turned my head to look at the woman who had approached me.

"Uh, yeah?"

"I'm sorry," She said, "Harry and Vic always seem to be busy out there. I was told that you might be able to help me?"

Denny was still picking at trays and popping bites of food into his mouth when I glanced over at him. Catering staff was cleaning up but also carrying fresh cases of drinks and ice outside to top off the troughs. Obviously, like everyone else, they didn't expect the party to end anytime soon.

"I can try?" I said as I rinsed my hands, shut off the water, and reached for a dishtowel.

"I'm Katie," She said.

Once my hands were dry, I took the hand she offered to me in greeting.

"Hi," I said, "Russ. But, uh, you knew that."

She laughed. "I was just wondering if you knew when Bang Bang would be here?"

Why does everyone keep asking me that? I'm not her freaking manager.

"No," I said, "I really don't know. I thought she'd be here by now, doing a show. Or enjoying the party, I guess?"

Katie sighed.

"I guess I'll text my sitter and see if she can stay later," She said. "I really wanted to talk to your uncles and see Bang Bang perform one last time."

"I hate to say it, but I'm starting to wonder if Bang Bang is even going to show up." I cringed.

"Oh, no."

"Bang Bang always shows up, one way or another. She's just known for being fashionably late. She likes to make an entrance," Denny said, his mouth full of whatever he had yanked off one of the trays.

I couldn't help but grin over at Denny. He hadn't even looked over at us when he injected himself into the conversation; he had just continued chewing and picking at the food on the trays. Denny might have been one of the most talkative people I knew, but he was also one of the sunniest people I'd met in a while. Besides, people who enjoy food are the best people.

"You think?" Katie glanced over at him and then back to me.

I shrugged. "Probably. I just can't speak for her is all."

"Okay," She said, looking slightly unsure. "It's just, I don't want to leave, but...well, sitters, you know?"

I didn't know, but I nodded and smiled as if I did.

"It's just," She continued, "your uncles and Bang Bang mean so much to me is all. I didn't want to leave without saying a few words to your uncles—and if I could see Bang Bang perform once more, it would be perfect."

My first thought was to just reassure Katie that Bang Bang would eventually show up if she could just be patient— and solve the problem with her sitter. It really wasn't in my nature to pry in the personal business of a stranger. However, after the dalliance with Denny in the garage and the fireworks display, I felt like maybe I should start acting out of character more often. It couldn't make my situation worse.

Could it?

"Oh?" It was the only way I knew how to dig further into her business without sounding downright nosy.

"Bang Bang and your uncles are why I'm here today," Katie said, grinning from ear to ear.

"At—at the party?"

Denny snorted with laughter. Katie chuckled along.

"Well," She said, "that too, I suppose. They did invite me. But no. I meant standing here alive and healthy."

"How so?" I was getting to be an expert at minding other people's business.

"Well," Katie glanced around, as though making sure no one else besides me was being nosy, "a few years ago, I...well, I was in the shelter. *The women's shelter.* My ex-husband...it wasn't a good situation. And I had two little ones. Still do, I guess. They're not much taller than my hip now."

"Okay," I said to show I was following along.

"Well," She continued, "I couldn't just live at the shelter forever with two little ones, right?"

"Right."

"So, Katie said, "I was out looking for jobs, and the library was one of the places hiring. Well, when I showed up to apply for a job, I guess I didn't look too professional. I didn't have much with me at the shelter. The clothes I'd been able to get from the house before I took off weren't really professional or anything. I didn't have any makeup. I probably looked a hot mess and like I had no business showing up *anywhere* looking for a job, let alone a library."

Katie laughed at this, so I did, too.

"They weren't as mean as they could have been about it," Katie continued, "but they made it clear I wasn't what they looking for."

"Ouch."

"Ouch is right," Katie said. "I was completely lost. I was sitting outside of the library on one of the benches, wondering what to do next, then suddenly, there was this man in a dress sitting next to me!"

Katie's eyes seemed to sparkle as she looked up at me. Then she seemed to have a thought.

"Sorry," She said, "that probably sounded homophobic, or, or—"

I waved her off with a smile.

"Well," Katie continued nervously, "it was Bang Bang. I guess he—*she?*"

I nodded.

"*She* had seen what had happened," Katie said. "She had been there doing one of her Drag Queen Reading Hours?

Well, she talked to me for a minute, told me a few jokes—*that I could never repeat*—listened to my story—held my hand as I cried—then she told me she could help. I don't know why I agreed—I just felt like I had known her all my life. Bang Bang just...well, she felt like an old friend. So, I decided to trust her."

"Oh, yeah?"

"She took me over to *A Straight Line*—back in the room where they get gussied up for the shows?" Katie said. "She did my makeup, my hair, put me in a new outfit—*it was a little ostentatious, but better than what I had*—and took me back to the library. We were sitting out in the car, outside of the library, and I just didn't know if marching back in there after being told to get lost was such a good idea. Bang Bang just looked at me and said: *Honey, where there's a drag queen, there's a way.* Then she walked up to that counter with me, spoke to the librarian on my behalf, and presented me like I was a prize sheep at the county fair!"

Katie laughed.

"I was so nervous!" Katie gasped. "I just knew Bang Bang was going to get us into trouble!"

"I can imagine." I chuckled.

"But Mrs. Johnson," Katie said," you know, the librarian? She hired me on the spot just at Bang Bang's word.

Well, and the fact that she showed I could clean up nicely. I had a job! I tell you, I was completely bowled over."

"That's amazing."

"I know, right?" Katie absolutely glowed with happiness at the memory. "Then, when I was falling on hard times and not making ends meet while trying to get my divorce—Bang Bang presented me to your uncles. They found me some side work. At Bethany's restaurant? Bussing tables and waitressing in the evenings? Helped me pay for my lawyer."

"Wow."

"If it weren't for Bang Bang and your uncles, I don't know where I'd be right now," Katie said. "They knew I was in a bad spot, but they trusted that I was the kind of person who didn't mind hard work to get out of a bad spot. I got out of the shelter, out from under that shit ex-husband—they saved my life."

I just stared at her.

"Two years ago," Katie held up her ring adorned finger, "your uncle Vic introduced me to a guy he knew who worked over at Lamont's Auto Yard. Joe and I just celebrated our first anniversary. He's outside enjoying the free drinks. My kids just adore him. They don't even miss their worthless ass daddy who hasn't paid one bit of his child support. Not that we need it anymore. I just—I can't believe that Harry and Vic won't be down at *A Straight Line* anymore. Or that I might never get to see Bang Bang perform again. I had to be here tonight so I could thank them one last time. Just in case our paths don't cross again."

For a few moments, I just stared at Katie, unsure of what to say.

"You never know," I said finally, "Bang Bang might still do a show from time to time. The new owners would be stupid not to invite her in every now and again."

"Ain't that the truth?" Katie laughed as she swatted at my arm. "They'd have to be downright stupid."

I smiled. "And Harry and Vic are always here. I know they'd love having any of their friends stop by to catch up."

"You know," Katie said, "I guess you're right. I was getting worked up over nothing."

"But," I said, "if you wait around, I'm sure you'll be able to talk to them. Maybe even catch Bang Bang's performance. Just tell your sitter how important tonight is to you. They'll understand."

"You're right about that, too!" Katie exclaimed. "And what's a few more dollars for a sitter if I get the opportunity, right?"

I gave her a smile and a nod. Katie patted my arm and headed towards the back door.

"You know," She said, turning to look at me, "I still don't know why Bang Bang took a chance on me—or your uncles for that matter—but I'm sure glad they did."

"That's just what they do," Denny said, still focusing on the trays.

I looked over at him.

"Sorry?" Katie said.

"They sprinkle a little queer magic dust everywhere they go," Denny responded, still not looking up from the trays.

Katie laughed. "Well, I'm glad they had a handful for me. God knows I needed it."

Then, with a smile powered by the memories she had shared, Katie turned on heel and marched outside. To call her sitter, I imagined.

God, I hope Bang Bang shows up soon.

"Do you ever stop eating?" I teased Denny.

"Talking and eating are what I do best." He shrugged.

"Well, the thing in the garage was a third thing," I said.

Denny looked up from the trays, his mouth stretched with food, and smiled at me. The effect was comical, so I allowed myself to laugh. Having complimented him on *his skills* in the garage, Denny was distracted from the food, finally chewing what was in his mouth so he could swallow. Then he sauntered around the kitchen island, his chest puffed out, and approached me.

"I'm also a good dancer." He crowed.

I didn't want to tell him "no" once again, so I changed the subject.

"You seem so sure that Bang Bang will show up," I said. "Why? I mean, I've never known Bang Bang to show up this late for a performance. She was always on stage at the exact moment she was supposed to be whenever I'd catch a show."

"She was never late." He agreed.

"And, I mean, maybe I never spent much personal time with Bang Bang—no one but the elders seem to really know her in that way," I said, "but she never struck me as someone who was this freaking fashionably late."

"That's true."

"So," I said, "why are you so sure?"

Denny grinned.

"Maybe I know something you don't know?" He suggested.

"You and Bang Bang best friends?" I chuckled.

"I wouldn't go *that* far," Denny said.

"Then why, damnit?" I nudged him.

"I just have a feeling." He shrugged. "Bang Bang always comes through. And I know she would never leave Harry and Vic high and dry. She certainly wouldn't do it on a night when all the elders are here to see it. They'd bring it up and give her hell about it any time they saw her from here until eternity."

"True." I agreed. "I just…"

"What?" Denny urged me on.

"I guess I need a sprinkling of her queer magic, too." I shrugged. "Bang Bang always makes things better."

Denny smiled.

"Yeah," He said. "Harry and Vic have done a great job, but it's not really a *great* party until Bang Bang shows up. It's certainly not as queer as it can be until she shows up."

"Agreed."

"You know," Denny leaned in, and at first, I thought he was trying to kiss me, but at the last minute, he held back, "you could use another drink."

"Well," I said, "if you're buying?"

He winked. "I think I might know where we can score a reasonably priced beverage."

"Oh, yeah? Do you—"

We both jumped at the sound of hoots and hollers as a gaggle of younger—and surprisingly, *shirtless*—gay men our age poured into the kitchen. Denny and I were parted like the Red Sea as the men infested the space like a hoard of cockroaches. Cupboards were swung open as the men chattered incessantly about "finding the booze." My first reaction was to angrily demand who these men thought they were, just marching into someone's house and going through their kitchen cabinets. However, over the din, I caught one of the men, some guy in tight blue jeans, cowboy boots, with a rainbow kerchief tied around his neck say: *"Harry said the 'good tequila' was in the cabinet by the fridge."*

Ah. The elders had sent the youngers to do their bidding.

Denny and I just gave each other confused smiles as we stood there, shirtless men dashing about around and between us. Liquor bottles were pulled out of cabinets, "hoots" and "whoops" were made, and men started heading back outside with their plunder. As the last shirtless man—a guy with the largest pecs I'd ever seen and more abs than I could count at first glance—dashed between Denny and me, I spotted a giant bottle of Patrón in his hand. When his eyes caught me standing there, he stopped abruptly in front of me, the tequila cradled in his arm at his side like a baby.

"Are you Russy?" He asked.

He actually had on body glitter.

Oh, honey. Country gays.

"Russ?" I didn't intend for it to sound like a question.

The man smiled and held out his hand. Tentatively, I slid mine into his. My whole body shook as the muscled shirtless guy waggled my arm like I was some inflatable creature outside of a car lot.

"Michael," He said a little too loudly.

From the smell of beer coming off of him, it was easy to figure out why he was having a problem with volume control.

"Russ," I repeated stupidly.

"Harry and Vic said I might find you in here," He said. *"Just look for the scrawny guy with glasses."*

"Wow." I looked over at Denny.

He was laughing like an asshole.

Obviously, the drunken-shirtless-muscled guy hadn't figured out he shouldn't actually repeat the way my uncles had described me to him. Well, probably not my *uncles*. The description had probably come from just Harry.

"Vic recommended me for my job over at the station," The guy—*Michael*—said.

"The station?" I asked.

"Officer Michael Hadsford." His chest puffed out proudly.

Considering the size of his chest, that was saying something.

"You're a police officer?" I asked, one eyebrow raising on its own.

"Hey," He said, his hand finally letting go of mine, "we all have to have a day job, right?"

"True," I said. "Just don't arrest anyone tonight."

I was only half-joking.

Michael laughed. "Short of someone getting murdered, I wouldn't ruin this party by arresting anyone for anything. I wouldn't do that to your uncles. They're both the best guys I know!"

I wondered how many beers I'd have to drink before shouting became my standard conversation setting.

"Likewise, I'm sure," I said neutrally.

Michael "whooped" and headed for the door, the tequila held securely in the crook of his arm.

"This party was so worth taking a vacation day," He shouted over his shoulder before dashing out the back door.

Finally, the door was shut, and Denny and I were left in virtual silence, save for the muffled sound of the music outside. The two of us just grinned at each other, amused at what had just transpired. I knew why Denny was grinning—I think. We had just witnessed a bunch of shirtless guys, who weren't so bad to look at, marching through the kitchen, close enough to touch if we had wanted. And they probably wouldn't have minded one bit. That's always something to smile about. I, on the other hand, was smiling because of the entire evening. Stories about my uncles, Bang Bang, food, beer, music, *a blowjob*, lesbians who could match Harry quip for quip, and then a parade of shirtless men. The whole night was ridiculous.

I loved it.

"I guess it's coming to the part of the evening where shots are in order?" I laughed.

Denny pulled his phone out of his pocket long enough to glance at it.

"It's nearly midnight," He said, slipping his phone away once again.

"Jeez." I shook my head. "Time slips away."

"Hey," Denny said, "do you…do you want my number? Ya' know…for another night? Just so tonight's not the only night we…hang out or whatever? Guys always have to eat dinner. Or see a movie. Maybe we could do that together sometime?"

I didn't want to go with my gut reaction to say "no" as firmly as possible. That gut reaction had been my go-to for so many months. Instead, I decided to fight it a little.

"Let's see how the night ends," I said. "Good enough?"

"Good enough," He said. "Another question?"

"Sure."

"Wanna go do shots with a bunch of shirtless guys, elder gays, and aged lesbians?" He grinned wickedly.

"And the younger lesbians?"

"And all the in-betweeners?"

"Let's go," I said.

Denny smiled and gestured towards the back door. Maybe I wasn't ready to commit to a dance, or a phone number so that we could have dinner at some future date—but I could commit to Patrón. I'm not made of steel, after all.

Chapter 9
The Wheels on the Bus

Denny and I tapped our cups together and slammed back the tequila, and the dozens of other partygoers surrounding us followed suit. *Raise Your Glass* by Pink had been set to play by Bird so that he could join us in our circle of hard liquor and Red Solo cups. Harry and Vic had actual shot glasses in the house, but they certainly didn't have enough to go around for everyone at the party. Instead, Michael—the shirtless police officer with a night off—had drunkenly poured tequila into the plastic cups for everyone. One look into my cup let me know that I was going to be slamming what was considerably more than a standard shot of tequila. However, it was getting late in the evening, peak party time, and I knew that I was way behind in the Buzzed Department compared to everyone else. Even the elders looked lit, so I knew that Denny and I had to do *something* to fit in with the rest of the revelers. If slamming more tequila than advisable was the way, so be it.

Then, as if one of the massive shots of tequila wasn't enough to take down a small horse, Michael, and other party attendees in possession of liquor bottles, began filling cups again. My brain was telling me that another shot was possibly a bad idea, but my heart told me to have a little fun. Besides, I hadn't had hardly anything to drink all night, and my belly was full of carbs. A little liquor wasn't going to be the end of me. *I hoped.* I looked around, already with my gut warm and my head tingly from the first shot, and smiled at the people gathered around us as Pink's party anthem played.

At first glance, I noticed that drag queens had shown up—which made my eyes dart around, looking for Bang Bang amongst the throngs of feather boas and sky-high hair. It wasn't too hard to find each of the drag queens in the crowd. With the high heels and flashy, big hair, they were all easy to find and identify as someone other than Bang Bang. My heart sunk a little when I realized that Bang Bang was not amongst the partygoers so late in the evening. Obviously, she had decided that showing up for the final hurrah just wasn't for her. I tried to remind myself that Denny had been so positive that Bang Bang would show up, but I wasn't so sure he wasn't just being overly optimistic. If she was going to come to the party and perform as promised, the window of time was closing.

"*Hey!*" Denny caught my attention.

I looked back at him to see a bottle of some liquid moving towards my cup. Forcing a smile onto my face, I held my cup next to Denny's so that the shirtless guy with the bottle could pour us another round. Everyone around us was rowdy, dancing in place to the song, but they waited patiently for everyone to have their cups ready for the next shot before taking their own. This was a group activity, obviously, and decorum had to not just be respected but observed. Once seemingly everyone had a second round of shots poured, the music suddenly stopped.

Over a hundred confused faces turned towards the DJ booth, wondering why the drinking music had been turned off. A glimmer of hope shot through me, thinking that maybe Bang Bang had finally arrived. Instead, I saw Vic and Harry standing up by the DJ booth with Bird, who had obviously been the one to shut off the music. I hated to admit that I was a little disappointed to see it was my uncles who had caused a stop to the activity instead of the arrival of everyone's favorite regional celebrity, but I forced myself to smile.

As the crowd grew quiet—which is an arduous task for a bunch of liquored-up queers—Harry and Vic smiled out at all of us. They both had Red Solo cups in hand, so obviously they were also doing shots with all of us. Standing in the center of the group of people with Denny, I hadn't seen them when we took our first shots. I had assumed they had chosen to sit out the silly activity. Of course, the elder gays knew all about taking shots. It's not like us younger gays had invented the activity, after all.

Is that weed I smell?

What will Officer Michael Hadsford think?

*Or is this **really** a night off for him?*

Once the crowd was silent, save for a few chuckles and drunken giggles, Vic spoke up:

"Harry and I don't want to stop the festivities for long," Vic announced loudly, "but we wanted to take this opportunity to thank our community for coming out tonight. We can't tell all of you how much it means to us to have all of our gay, lesbian, bi, pan, allies, questioning, intersex, trans, drag, ace—"

Harry whispered something quickly to Vic.

"—and our nonbinary and non-gender-conforming brothers, sisters, and they and thems with us tonight. And if I said any of that wrong or offended anyone, I'm sorry, but you can all fuck off."

Everyone in the crowd laughed uproariously.

"But regardless of whether or not you're LGBTQ-plus, or an ally—or, I guess, other—this has been a night we will never forget. Forty years ago, Harry and I opened *A Straight Line*—"

The crowd cheered so loudly it was deafening.

"—and forty years ago, we never imagined this day. To see all of the faces here—so many familiar ones, so many new ones, and even more beautiful in the diversity—it's a testament to how wonderful this community is. Our lives, the bar—all of it has been made possible by all of you. You've all made two tired old queers realize that their lives and their business meant something. We will always, *always*, be eternally grateful for that."

More cheers sounded, as well as claps, and "awwww's."

"So," Vic said, "thank you all. From the bottom of our hearts. We couldn't have asked for a better community or better lives. And it's thanks to all of you."

More claps and cheers.

Some people in the crowd snapped and shouted back: "*No! You!*"

Vic stepped back, offering Harry a chance to speak to the gathered masses. Harry, with Red Solo cup in hand, stepped forward, opened his mouth…and a short sob erupted. He slapped a hand over his mouth as tears appeared in his eyes. Everyone in the crowd made "aw" sounds as Harry collected himself. Then the claps began, urging him to speak. However, when Harry finally composed himself, he simply said:

"Oh, just thank you. Take your shots, you silly queers!"

Everyone laughed, smiles of gratitude on their faces, then held their cups out in salute to the founders of *A Straight Line*. Then we were all tossing our cups back, massive amounts of liquor finding their way down our gullets. Everyone cheered around me as I grimaced at realizing I had just downed half a cup's worth of whiskey.

That oughta do it. I thought to myself as I pulled the cup away from my mouth.

Let's Have a Kiki by Scissor Sisters was queued up by Bird, and the crowd around us went wild. I started to find my way through the crowd and off the dance floor area as everyone around me began dancing along to the song. As I expected, Denny caught up to me, his own empty cup in hand. I had nearly made it to the edge of the crowd before he reached out and hooked a hand through the crook of my elbow. I didn't turn to see what he wanted because I already knew what he was going to ask of me. And a dance was out of the question.

We had almost made our way to the edge of the crowd, getting slapped in the face accidentally by every color of feather boa imaginable and getting elbowed accidentally by sparkly queers covered in body glitter. I would never say anything to Harry, so he didn't freak out, but I was certain that at least one pair of Doc Martens had stomped on my toes accidentally. The last thing I needed, besides Denny pulling at my elbow, was to have Harry freak out that lesbians from upstate New York had come to exact their revenge on him.

Finally, when we had a little breathing room from the throngs of dancers, I eased up and let Denny's grip on my elbow stop me. He rounded my body, his hand slowly slipping away from my elbow, and he looked at me with a hopeful smile. The expression on his face—euphoric, slightly drunk, hopeful—almost like a puppy asking its new owner to love it—made it hard not to feel bad. However, I just wasn't ready to commit to anything. Not even something as simple as a dance. Exchanging blowjobs in a dark garage was one thing. In and out, mission accomplished. But committing to starting something new with some guy who was a virtual stranger was just too much. My heart wasn't ready for that yet.

"The night's waning," Denny said, "I'm still saving that dance."

"It's not really my song," I shouted over the music and the excited sounds coming from the people dancing nearby. "Maybe a different song? Later?"

"How much later?" He looked absolutely defeated.

"I don't know, I—"

"You just don't want to dance with me." His bottom lip jutted out.

I would have gotten pissed at the attempt to emotionally manipulate me if he hadn't looked so forlorn. Luckily, a familiar glittery chest flashed in the corner of my eye before I could say something that might be interpreted as rude by Denny. Officer Michael was dancing past us, his arms going in a million different directions, causing leftover liquor droplets to fly erratically from the cup held aloft in one of his hands. Quickly, I reached out and hooked my hand through the crook of his arm, pulling him towards us. It was no easy task, considering the man was nothing but solid muscle, but once he looked down at my hand and saw I was trying to get his attention, he helped me out by stepping over to us.

"*Officer Michael?*" I shouted over the music. "*Dance with Denny!*"

I gestured at Denny. Michael glanced over at him and smiled.

"*He loves this song!*" I shouted.

Officer Michael nodded his head, as though to say, "*why not?*" and held his hand out to Denny. For a second, I thought Denny might throw his cup at me or curse at me. However, after a moment, he handed his empty cup to me for safe-keeping and took Officer Michael's hand. The policeman let out a "whoop" and pulled Denny into the crowd, leaving me alone with two empty cups. I watched for a minute, Denny's and Michael's backs disappearing amongst the undulating sea of gyrating bodies, then turned away.

Why am I like this?

Once I found the nearest place to dispose of the empty cups, I zigzagged my way around the dance floor, dodging flailing bodies on the outer perimeter of the dance floor area and slapping away boas that swung at my face. When I got over to the DJ booth, Harry and Vic were still standing there, their own red cups in hand, grinning and chatting animatedly with each other. It was obvious by the expressions on their faces that the party was a success, and their days had been perfect. I couldn't let myself be dour around them. Ruining one of the most perfect evenings in their lives would have been unforgivable, even for a miserable bastard such as myself.

"Hey," I said, somehow loudly enough to be heard over the music.

Harry and Vic turned to me, looking surprised to see me standing before them. I wasn't sure if they were shocked that I hadn't locked myself in my room for the night, or they had just forgotten that I was even at the party, but my appearance had taken them by surprise.

"Russ!" Vic exclaimed. "Why aren't you dancing?"

I shrugged.

"Where's Denny?" Harry asked quickly.

"Why?" I grumbled.

"Well," Harry said, "I've seen you two together quite a bit tonight. I thought maybe the two of you would be dancing is all."

"Harry," Vic mumbled just loudly enough to be heard over the music.

"Well," Harry said, "when they disappeared into the garage together, I thought—"

My cheeks burned brightly—not at the fact that we'd been seen going into the garage together—but that what Uncle Harry thought we had been doing *was what we had been doing*. It was one thing to have my uncles see me milling about the party with Denny, even enjoying myself, I guess, around Denny. But to have them see us go into the garage together was a different matter. Casual sex isn't as taboo in the LGBTQ-plus community like it is in other communities, so it wasn't that I felt they would shame me. I just preferred that they never thought about me having sex. Ever. I never wanted to think about the sex *they* had.

"He's dancing with Officer Michael," I said, hoping that would end the discussion.

I gestured vaguely at the dance area.

Harry and Vic both glanced at everyone dancing, their faces dropping.

"Oh, Russy," Harry said, moving closer, "I'm so sorry. I thought—"

"I told him to," I cut him off.

"What?" Vic frowned.

"I didn't want to dance."

"That sounds like bullshit," Harry said.

"Harry," Vic repeated his warning.

Loving my Uncle Harry was never a problem. Loving my Uncle Vic was never a problem, either, for that matter. But from time to time, I just wanted to tell Harry to go fuck himself. How dour I'd been the last several months, and how stubborn I was being in general, had not escaped me. I was well aware of my problems—even if I didn't know how to fix them. I didn't need Harry to throw that in my face. I didn't need anyone to remind me that I had my head firmly up my own ass. I just needed time to figure out how to extricate it.

Don't tell him to go fuck himself. I thought. *It's their big night.*

Harry waved a hand towards the crowd like shooing away a fly.

"Just go out there and cut in," He said. "I may not know a lot, but I know that boy won't mind you cutting in. He's been eyeing you all night."

"Harry," Vic said, "leave Russ alone now. Tonight's just supposed to be fun. We don't need you playing matchmaker."

"I'm just saying that he's been following Russ around like a puppy dog all night," Harry said. "Obviously, he's interested in getting to know him better. *One dance won't hurt him any.* Just go out there, tap him on the shoulder, and—"

"*We're looking for Harry and Victor Thomas!*" A static-y, mechanical voice suddenly rang out over the crowd.

Harry, Vic, and I all jumped at the sound of the announcement, which was obviously coming from a bullhorn, but it took Bird and everyone dancing a little longer to catch up. Like a record on a turntable that is slowly running out of power, Bird shut the music off, and everyone stopped dancing. Vic, Harry, and I all were looking over the crowd, trying to figure out what was going on and where the screeching of the bullhorn had come from in the backyard. Due to the confusion at the music suddenly stopping and everyone that had been dancing stopping, there was chaos for several moments. Then the loud announcement came again.

"*We need to find Harry and Victor Thomas!*" The mechanical voice rang out again.

Immediately, I could tell that the announcement was coming from the side of the house closest to the garage, which was across the yard from where Harry, Vic, and I stood near the patio. I gave my uncles a nudge and flicked my head in the direction of the garage. My uncles grabbed each other's hands as I started to lead them through the crowd so that we could find out who had been using a bullhorn to try and get their attention.

In my mind, I just knew that it was going to be the cops waiting for us. It was well after midnight, loud music was playing, a bunch of queer people of all different colors were gathered with alcohol—that was a recipe for "here comes the cops." Murmurs started to tear through the crowd as everyone slowly started to figure out what was going on and began turning to watch the three of us making our way towards the garage. Once we got through the sea of people and exited the crowd by the garage, my suspicions were confirmed. Two officers, in full uniform, were standing by the corner of the house. The officer in front, a tall, built guy, had a bullhorn held in one hand, dangling at his side. I glanced over at Harry and Vic as we approached them. I was nervous to see the cops, but Harry and Vic just looked curious.

A couple of older gay men probably don't get too frazzled when cops show up at a party. I thought to myself.

The officers' eyes landed on our trio.

"Are you Harry and Vic Thomas?" The officer with the bullhorn asked, just loudly enough for everyone at the party to hear.

Everyone was staring at us and the cops in wonder. You could have heard a pin drop.

"That's us, yes," Vic answered for them. "What can we help you with?"

"I'm Officer Johnson, and this is Officer Smith," The lead officer announced, "Littleburg Police Department."

"*Oh, shit.*" Someone far back in the crowd hissed.

I was pretty sure it was Officer Michael Hadsford. The corner of my mouth turned up slightly.

"We kind of assumed that, officer," Harry said. "The uniforms gave it away. You guys must be new. Don't recognize you at all."

I wanted to reach over and nudge Harry in the arm for being smart-alecky to the officers who had obviously shown up about a noise complaint. Hell, maybe they were going to charge everyone with obscenity. We were all queers—or *queer adjacent*. Instead of getting upset with Harry's smart mouth, Officer Johnson, the one with the bullhorn, just smiled.

"We've been sent here to pick you up, sirs." He said.

"What?" Uncle Vic looked over at me. "We're not going to jail. We've done nothing wrong."

"What's going on?" I couldn't stop myself. "My uncles are just throwing a party because they sold their bar. They didn't do anything wrong."

Harry and Vic motioned for me to be quiet.

Officer Johnson held his hands up defensively.

"We're not here to pick you up to take you to jail, sirs," Officer Johnson said.

Murmurs went through the crowd again. I could understand everyone's confusion. Why were officers from the Littleburg Police Department here to "pick them up" if not to take them to jail? Where were they taking them?

"We've been sent by Bang Bang Baisemoi," Officer Johnson seemed a little uncomfortable saying the name, "to pick you up. There seems to be a performance you've been invited to see."

The murmuring in the crowd began again, but this time it wasn't from confusion; it was everyone overjoyed at the announcement that the cops weren't at the party to ruin everyone's good time.

"We have four school buses out front," Officer Smith spoke up, "in case you want to bring your friends along to see the performance as well?"

Murmurs weren't what followed. Everyone in the crowd began clapping and cheering. Harry and Vic, completely dumbfounded, just looked at each other with goofy grins. Everyone around us was practically jumping up and down with excitement as a smile bloomed on my face.

Bang Bang hadn't decided to skip out on my uncles after all.

Instead of trying to use the bullhorn to be heard over the crowd, the officers motioned for Harry and Vic to follow them out to the front of the house. Both of my uncles looked completely dumbfounded, but with a nudge from me, they let the officers lead them away from the backyard.

"*Everyone follow us!*" Harry shouted over his shoulder as the officers led the way.

More cheers erupted as I, along with over a hundred partygoers, fell in line behind my uncles.

When we got around the side of the house to the front lawn, we were greeted with four long yellow school buses, each with a drag queen in complete party regalia in the driver's seats. They all waved and motioned for people to begin piling onto the buses. The crowd surged forward once the officers got Harry and Vic on the first bus, seated behind the drag driver, and the first three buses quickly filled up. Somehow, in my amusement and amazement, I didn't realize what was happening, so I wasn't able to get on the first bus to ride with Harry and Vic. Instead, I was left with the stragglers at the back of the crowd, along with Felix, Frank, Denny, Bethany, and a handful of the younger queer people who had been invited to the party.

All of us looked at each other, realizing we'd get left behind if we didn't get our wits about us and hurriedly piled into the fourth bus. Felix and Bethany took the seat behind the driver, and I fell into the seat across the aisle from them. I wasn't sure if I was happy or annoyed when Denny climbed onto the bus and crawled over me to sit by the window in the bench seat next to me, but I decided to try and be pleasant. Frank and the remaining partygoers filed in quickly after us and took empty seats, ready to get to Bang Bang's performance.

Suddenly, a thought struck me. Denny had been so sure that Bang Bang would make an appearance, even when I was certain that all hope was lost.

"*Hey,*" I said, leaning closer to him, "*did you know about this?*"

Denny smiled. "*Grandpa might have mentioned something.*"

I returned his smile, then turned to look at Felix sitting next to Bethany across the aisle. Felix looked over at me, gave me a quick wink, then turned his attention back to the driver in front of him. I sat up, looking out of the front of the window for the cop cars that were obviously going to lead us to…wherever we were headed, but couldn't find them. I began to wonder if Officers Johnson and Smith were actually officers at all, or two queer men Bang Bang had employed to come pick everyone up from Harry's and Vic's place. It would be just like Bang Bang to do such a thing. Make everyone think they're in trouble before inviting them to a performance.

"Let's go, Nita!" Felix barked happily at the driver.

"You ain't gotta tell me twice, baby!" She cooed back, and, with a very well-manicured hand, she used the lever to shut the bus doors.

The buses ahead of us started to surge forward, so Nita—who I suddenly recognized as one of Bang Bang's friends, *Nita Mann*—pressed her high-heeled foot to the gas. Then we were off. From behind us on the bus, drunken younger gays started to sing:

The wheels on the bus go 'round and 'round, 'round and 'round…

"*How's this for that queer magic?*" Denny asked, giving me a nudge in the side.

Chapter 10
A Straight Line

Nita Mann wasn't exactly the most adept bus driver I had ever encountered, but the fact that she was operating a giant steering wheel with red candy-coated nails, pushing the brake and gas pedals in six-inch heels, as her wig brushed against the bus ceiling, made me feel that she was doing a great job. Even though she seemed to hit every pothole down every road we traveled, and she was liberally using the word "shit" with each occurrence, she wasn't half bad. Felix, Bethany, Denny, and I all had our hands clamped to our seats. The gays in the back of the bus were sliding back and forth in their seats, hooting and hollering, and singing silly songs like they were on the bus on their way to grade school for their first day.

Once we had made it off of the country road that led out to Harry's and Vic's house and we made it to the highway, I was able to pry my fingers off of the seat and relax. Nita was a much better driver on a road that was paved well and didn't have quite as many potholes and turns. Driving in a straight line on a highway was definitely more Nita's speed. With the bus moving more steadily and with us not being jostled so much in our seats, I turned to look at Bethany and Felix, who were deep in discussion with each other behind the driver. Of course, I now knew that Felix had been in on whatever plan Bang Bang had concocted, but I was desperate to know more.

"So," I spoke across the aisle, "Bang Bang had this planned all along?"

Felix stopped talking to Bethany, and they both looked over at me.

"Whatever are you talking about?" Felix asked.

"Oh, give it up, Felix," I said. "It's obvious now. Besides, your grandson sold you up the river."

I jabbed a thumb over my shoulder.

"I didn't say anything for certain," Denny said.

"He would never rat me out." Felix winked at Denny.

"Either way, this was really nice of Bang Bang," I said. "And you. I know Harry and Vic are thrilled."

And my mood's greatly improved as well. Even if this isn't about me.

Denny gave my shoulder a squeeze as Nita continued to steer the bus down the highway towards our destination.

"Where are we going?" I asked loudly so Nita could hear me.

Nita's mouth opened to respond, but she was cut off.

"It's a secret!" Felix interjected. "Everyone will just have to wait and find out. Stop bothering the driver, anyway.

We don't want to crash with a bus full of drunk queers. I can only imagine the headlines!"

Bethany brayed with laughter.

Obviously, her mind had conjured up what those supposed headlines would say.

"Just enjoy the ride," Denny said from over my shoulder.

"I bet you tell all the boys that." I teased.

Jesus Christ. What was wrong with me?

Just knowing that Bang Bang was coming through with her performance that she had promised for Vic and Harry, and the fact that we were all on buses on the way to that performance, had me giddy. Denny just laughed at my remark and nudged me in the back with an elbow.

"You know," Bethany said, "this is just like Bang Bang. Her whole life is one damn performance. That isn't a criticism, mind you. Remember that time they tried to shut the bar down in those early years—right after Harry and Vic started serving food?"

"What?" I leaned further across the aisle to hear Bethany better.

The younger queers at the back of the bus were attempting to sing the entire *Rent* soundtrack, and while it was festive, it wasn't conducive to us having a conversation.

"The damn City Council sent the police over to the bar one night to shut them down." Bethany turned in her seat to look at me.

Felix nodded at me over her shoulder.

"Why?" I gasped.

I could feel Denny had shifted behind me to look over my shoulder so he could listen to Bethany's story.

"Someone was telling everyone in town that the boys were giving blowjobs and *committing other depraved acts* in the bar's bathrooms," Felix said.

Bethany nodded. "This was the late eighties—little town in the Midwest? A gay bar was one thing, but knowing that the gays were actually having sex? That just couldn't be tolerated. I mean, granted, sex in public is a crime of obscenity and all—"

"Only if you're doing it right." Felix quipped.

Denny and I chuckled nervously.

"—but someone just had to go around telling everyone that. Once the mayor and City Council—and then the police—caught wind of it, well, they planned to come in, check it out for themselves, arrest anyone caught doing anything *obscene*—and shutter the doors for good," Bethany said. "They didn't just intend to ticket your uncles and maybe give them a fine, no. They were going to use it as a way to get rid of *the queers* for good."

"That's ridiculous!" I gasped. "All that for a rumor?"

"It wasn't a rumor!" Felix proclaimed. "Of course, the boys were having sex with each other in the bathrooms. That's what a gay bar bathroom is for!"

"What?" I laughed.

"It's just what we do," Felix said with a wave of his hand. "It's a longstanding tradition in the gay community. It's part of our heritage. It's nothing to be ashamed of, Russy. Two consenting adult men getting their rocks off? It's sweet."

"Well, I don't know about *sweet*," I said, forcing myself not to look over my shoulder at Denny, "but I guess it's nice that there's a pot for every lid?"

"Fair enough," Felix said. "But the rumor wasn't a rumor. Someone decided to blab their big mouth about the bar and all the fun we had. The breeders couldn't stand for the queers having any kind of freedom or fun."

Bethany nodded. "Well, the cops showed up one night. *All of 'em.* Granted, in Littleburg, that's just a handful, but they were ready to come in, check things out, and haul people away. The bar would've been kaput after that."

"What's that got to do with Bang Bang?" I asked the logical question.

"As soon as we saw those flashing lights in the front windows of the bar," Bethany said, "Bang Bang gathered up every queen in the bar and went out front to greet the cops.

They all joined arms and made a can-can line, kicking their heels up and singing show tunes."

"That made the cops go away?" I laughed. "I don't believe this story at all."

"Of course, it didn't make them go away," Felix said.

"Nope." Bethany agreed. "But it gave the rest of us time to go clear the bathrooms out. So, when the cops finally got past the queens and into the bar, everyone was dancing, enjoying their drinks, or otherwise behaving like normal bar patrons. The only person in the bathroom when they checked it out was some kid taking a leak."

"That was brave of Bang Bang," I said.

"Sure, it was," Felix said. "She could've gotten herself arrested for interfering in an investigation or something. Any charge those cops wanted to throw at her, I suppose. Between the four of us, I think they were afraid to put a queen in handcuffs and frisk her. They might find something besides a weapon strapped to her."

Bethany cackled.

"I wouldn't be shocked if Bang Bang had a weapon on her at all times, actually. At least a straight razor." I laughed.

"You aren't kidding," Bethany said.

Denny was resting his chin on my shoulder, which didn't make me *exactly* comfortable, as he listened to the elders tell the story.

"Anyway," Felix continued, "after that night was over, Bang Bang ended up buying the field behind the bar. You know the one that's still empty except for that old Airstreamer?"

"Yeah?" Denny and I both responded.

"Well," Felix grinned, "now any of the boys that want to have a little fun had somewhere to go. It's a trailer on private property. If they wanna go get their rocks off in a trailer on Bang Bang's property—*in privacy*—there ain't nothing the cops, the City Council—*nobody*—can do about it."

"Of course," Bethany said, "they tried for a few years after she bought the land to search it, but without reports of a crime and a warrant—and no one giving them permission— there was nothing they could do about it."

"Bang Bang to the rescue!" Felix crowed and pumped a fist in the air.

"She wasn't going to let some homophobic officials tell the boys they couldn't slip each other the pickle if they wanted to," Bethany said. "She made sure that the longstanding tradition in our community of casual sex with strangers in a dark room could continue!"

Bethany and Felix gave each other "high-fives," which I hadn't seen anyone do outside of a football stadium in years.

"I don't know," I said, biting at my lip, "it is kind of untoward, isn't it? The having sex with strangers in public thing, right?"

Denny's chin tensed on my shoulder.

"What do you mean?" Felix asked.

"I mean, isn't it *kind of* obscene?" I suggested though I wasn't sure I believed anything I was saying. "It is kind of salacious to just meet some person, drag them into the bathroom in a bar, and go to town on each other?"

"You listen here, you little shit," Felix said, nudging Bethany out of the way so he could lean further across the aisle. "You come from a long line of queers—of all different shapes, sizes, flavors, and colors—who have faced every form of oppression you could imagine. Sometimes the only way we could live freely and fully was by taking care of our needs in backrooms, bathrooms, and back alleys. We had to do what we had to do in order to live our lives honestly. To be with the people we loved. We couldn't just set up house somewhere and have people be okay with it."

Bethany was nodding furiously.

"We had to be discreet. Just so we wouldn't be jailed, beaten—hell, killed—just because our love looks different on the outside. Giving some guy a blowjob in a bar bathroom is part of our heritage. It's not *salacious*. A lot of people who belong to our community want to deny so much of what makes it great—just because it doesn't fit in with *polite society* or doesn't fit what they think the aesthetic should be. Even though now, at least in this country, two men or two women can get married, get a house, and live their lives openly a little more safely than in the past, it's still an act of rebellion to be a queer. It's still dangerous to be queer, no matter what the laws say."

I chewed at my lip as I listened.

"When a guy gives a blowjob in a bathroom, sure, they're having fun," Felix said with a wave of his hand, "but they're almost paying homage to where we came from. They're on their knees thanking whatever power there is that we've come this far. For all that we've come from, we still have a long way to go. It's downright frustrating. But sometimes you have to kick up your heels and celebrate how far we've come. That's what we do. We're queers. In the darkest of times, in better times, we kick up our heels and have a good time when we can. Because the dark times need some light. And you never know how long the good times will last. So...suck a dick every chance you get, Russy. A lot of queers have suffered for your right to do so."

Felix sat back in his seat, and Denny's chin stopped digging so roughly into my shoulder. For a long moment, we were all silent. I felt like such a dick for even suggesting that what queers do in bar bathrooms from time to time was bad. It was even worse that I had said it to one of the elder gays who hadn't always had it as easy as I had. Sometimes, us younger queers forget what the queers who came before us have gone through. What they continue to go through as not just queers, but as older people. Often pushed aside by the next generation, like a lot of older people, forgotten, deemed "out of touch" or "not with it," all of their wisdom, experiences, and hardships—the battles they fought and lost, the wars they won for everyone that would come after them—they weren't appreciated enough.

You're a real shit, Russ.

"Well," Bethany said finally, "I would've said 'eat a pussy,' but I guess what Felix said is adequate enough."

That immediately broke the tension, and all four of us were laughing uproariously.

"Look at that!" Bethany joked. "I got three gays to laugh at a pussy joke!"

"Okay, okay." Felix slapped at her gently. "Just stop saying 'pussy,' would you?"

We continued to laugh, not just because we were glad that Bethany had wiped away the tension I had created with one question about bathroom blowjobs, but because it was funny. Also, the night was about celebrating Harry, Vic, and the little queer bar in the middle of America that could. There was no reason for any of us to be tense or pissed off. I smiled at the thought of Bang Bang, Harry, and Vic working so hard over the years to bring some joy to the life of queer people in Littleburg and the surrounding area for so many years. They had done such a good job that they were actually able to sell it off to another person who wanted to continue that tradition.

How was that not something to be joyous about, after all?

"Hey," I said as I glanced out the windshield in front of us, "we're going south through Littleburg."

Felix grinned.

A Straight Line was located off the highway on the south end of Littleburg.

"We sure are, sugar," Nita said as she steered.

"Nita!" Felix admonished her playfully.

"Oh, shut up," She growled playfully over her shoulder at Felix, "it's not like it would've been a secret much longer, you old queen. We're almost there!"

Sure enough, another glance out the windshield showed bright lights up ahead as we passed the last stop sign at the end of Main Street. A few miles down the road, every color of the rainbow was shining high into the sky, as though searchlights had been set up. In amazement, I wondered how *A Straight Line* had gone from a queer bar in a little midwestern town that didn't want it, to a business that the town would allow to put on such a display in the middle of the night. Of course, when I thought of all of the things that Bang Bang had done for Littleburg, and all of the things Harry and Vic had done for the community, it was no wonder that Littleburg finally came around.

"Is...is that the bar?" I gasped.

"Well, it ain't the Taj Mahal," Felix said.

"But it may as well be to us," Bethany added.

Up ahead of us, the first bus was slowing down in front of where all of the lights at the entrance of the bar were shining up into the sky. Then the second bus and the third, and finally, Nita slowed our bus down behind them. With her high-heeled foot, she somehow expertly applied the brakes on the bus and brought us to a stop behind the third bus, with just enough room to avoid a collision. Once the bus was at a full stop and she had shut it off—and all of the other buses had queers pouring out of them—Nita turned to look over the back of her seat at us.

"Okay, ya' bunch of drunken queens!" She shouted. "Any other ride you're getting from me tonight won't be on this damned bus!"

Everyone laughed and rose from their seats. Chaos was on full display outside of the bar as all of the people who had arrived on the buses waited outside. When I stepped off the bus, I could see Harry and Vic near the doors, where the two "cops"—Officers Johnson and Smith—were making everyone wait. Once the buses were unloaded, and the crowd had quieted down, Officer Johnson stepped up.

"Ladies and gentlemen," He announced loudly, "we'd like to welcome you, on behalf of Ms. Bang Bang Baisemoi, to *A Straight Line!*"

Then, much to everyone's delight, the "cops" ripped their shirts open, exposing chiseled pecs and abs. Hoots and hollers sounded from the crowd, as the two men in cop uniforms reached for the doors. Each of them took a handle and pulled the doors wide. Disco music greeted us all, and we cheered. Immediately, the crowd surged forth like a wave, and we were all pouring through the front doors of the bar. I lost sight of Harry and Vic as the crowd moved through the entrance in a giant undulation of bodies, but once I had managed to push my way inside, they were easy to spot.

Bang Bang had a platoon of queens at the bar serving drinks, tables and chairs set up, and the dance floor cleared out for anyone who wanted to kick up their heels. A table with two chairs had been set up at the edge of the dance floor, which was obviously intended for Harry and Vic. If there was any doubt about that, Felix and the other guys from The Flirtatious Five were leading them to the seats of honor. I smiled, realizing that all of the guys had obviously been in on Bang Bang's plan to get my uncles to the bar one last time before the new owners took charge. Simon and Phil had been left out of the scheme—

for obvious reasons. Of course, Denny had been clued in by Felix, so I found myself wanting to be hurt at being left out. However, I remembered that I had just recently moved in with Vic and Harry, so who had the time to pull me aside and tell me the secret plan?

Nearly half of the people in attendance were on the dance floor, dancing to some disco song I wasn't really familiar with, while nearly half were at the bar, driving the drag queens crazy with drink orders. From the look of things, the queens were simply shoving beers and shots at people, basically telling them to make do with what they gave them. I imagined that Bang Bang hadn't paid the queens to actually tend bar like professionals, so they were under no obligation to make anything fancy for anyone. Beer and shots would have to suffice.

Denny suddenly appeared at my side once again with two beers—gripped by the necks in one hand—and two shots—cradled in the palm of his other. With a laugh at his ability to get to the head of the drink line so quickly, I took one of the beers and one of the shot glasses from him. We tapped the shot glasses together and tossed them back. Tequila. And not the best. But I was perfectly fine with that. We set our shot glasses on a nearby table and tapped our beers together before taking a long drink off of them as well. Then the two of us turned towards the dance floor and watched everyone dancing from afar, the music so loud I could feel it in my bones. I imagined that both of my uncles would be saying "*huh?*" and "*what?*" a lot for days following the party. But they'd be smiling when they said it.

While we stood there, sipping our beers and watching everyone dance, I noticed out of the corner of my eye that Denny kept glancing at me. I knew that he wanted to remind me that he had been saving a dance for me, but I hoped he wouldn't. I just wanted to stand there and enjoy my drink and watch everyone having a good time—especially Harry and Vic. I didn't want to ruin the night by having too much fun with Denny. Months may have passed since my last relationship fell apart at the seams, but I just wasn't ready to give my heart hope. After a few minutes of the song that was playing, Denny seemed to realize that I wasn't going to dance, and just stood close by, his arm touching mine, as we watched everyone else having fun.

When the last few notes of the song tapered off, and silence took over the room, all of the lights suddenly went out. Several people gasped. A few screamed out. Others made sexual noises to be funny. I felt Denny's hand find mine at our sides, and his fingers slipped between mine. My first instinct was to pull away, but instead, I just grasped his hand back. It was dark. I didn't have to see him looking pleased, and he couldn't see the small smile that turned up the corners of my mouth, no matter how much I willed it not to happen.

After a few moments of darkness and everyone making rude sounds, a single spotlight came on in the dark. A large white circle appeared at the center of the stage that was just past the dance floor. Screams of excitement echoed through the bar when we all realized what the spotlight was focused on.

Bang Bang Baisemoi.

Chapter 11
Bang Bang Baisemoi

"Look at all of you drunk bitches." Bang Bang hissed at all of us reproachfully, her mouth turned up in a wicked, red-lipsticked smile.

Even from the back of the room, I could see her signature grin.

Everyone snapped and hollered for Bang Bang.

"Oh, shut the fuck up!" She waved us all off as she crossed her arms over her chest. "You all look a hot damn mess. Just look at all of you!"

We all laughed at the way she admonished us. We all knew that Bang Bang was just teasing.

"Drunk," She exclaimed. "Sweaty. Shirtless. Probably high."

Several whistles echoed through the crowd.

"And do I see...*body glitter?*" She held a hand over her eyes to peer out at the crowd. "Who took Simon's advice on how to dress for a party?"

Everyone laughed loudly—well, those who knew Simon laughed the hardest. I was certain, though I couldn't find him in the crowd, that Simon wasn't laughing. Phil was probably stifling laughter so that Simon wouldn't chew him a new asshole at home.

"Body glitter!" Bang Bang 'tsked'. "Ever hear the one about the two guys who were arrested at Michael's for dipping their testicles in the glitter?"

"*NOOOOO!*" The crowd shouted in unison.

"Well, I don't remember the entire story, but it was pretty nuts!" Bang Bang fake laughed and waved a hand at the crowd.

Everyone laughed, and I gripped Denny's hand tighter.

"I used to wear body glitter all the time, you know," Bang Bang announced, to which the audience did their part and pretended to be shocked. "No! It's true, it's true. I hate to admit it, but I, Bang Bang Baisemoi, used to be a body glitter *junkie!*"

Again, the crowd displayed disbelief. I joined in with the hollering like we were at a midnight viewing of *The Rocky Horror Picture Show*.

"My roommate used to get so mad at me!" She crowed. "I'd come home after nights out at the clubs—this was when I was in New York."

Bang Bang patted at her hair arrogantly, making everyone laugh.

"And I was too tired to clean myself off. Too tired to even take a shower. I'd just fall down asleep wherever I could.

Well, my roommate, he'd get so mad at the trail of glitter. The glitter on the floor. The glitter on the sofa. The glitter on the counters. He'd complain, complain, complain. So, I finally told him that I'd stop. That'd I'd give up my body glitter habit."

The crowd responded with a round of "no!"

"Yes. I did. So, when he went out to work one night, I mixed up a bucket of glue and glitter. Hung it right up over the front door of our apartment."

The crowd was laughing in anticipation.

"Hung it right up over the front for his return," Bang Bang said. "And then I stood there and waited. Sure enough, two hours later, he came home with a pocketful of cash. He opened that front door...*and I punched him right in his face.*"

Everyone laughed uproariously.

"Yes, I did." Bang Bang screamed at the crowd. "Yes, I did. I don't regret it one bit. The asshole had it coming. Tell me I can't wear body glitter. Wear your body glitter, boys. Be a hot damn mess! Be proud!"

More hoots and hollers.

"*What kind of job is only two hours a day?!?*" Someone shouted from the audience.

Everyone in the audience laughed.

Bang Bang leaned forward on the stage in the general direction from which the voice had come.

"Oh, you sweet summer child," She said.

Everyone laughed harder.

"If someone goes off to work and comes back two hours later with a pocket full of cash, they're either selling weed or ass, honey," She said, to which everyone laughed. "He was doing both."

The laughter swelled as Bang Bang worked the stage.

"Speaking of fucked up jobs," She said, "do you know what the mohel said to the prostitute?"

The crowd responded with a round of "no's" again.

"*You can keep the tip!*" Bang Bang screeched and slapped at her knee.

Again, more laughter rang out in the bar.

"Oh, my," Bang Bang sighed, "we have all the time in the world for dick jokes. And no one tells a dick joke like…"

"*A queen trying to hide one!*" The crowd, including me, shouted back.

"Oh!" Bang Bang clutched at her chest with joy. "My babies!"

Everyone cheered.

"But," Bang Bang peered out into the crowd towards Harry's and Vic's table, "this is a special performance for me tonight. And I guess it's not really a performance—*because I'm not getting fucking paid.*"

The crowd erupted with laughter once again.

"It's okay, it's okay." Bang Bang waved a dismissive hand. "Leave it to your two best friends to fuck with your bag and feel good about it, amirite?"

More hoots and hollers. I could see Harry and Vic over the crowd, and Harry was flipping Bang Bang off from their table, which made me smile.

"Now *that* will cost you, Harry." Bang Bang shouted at him. "I've *never* done *that* for free."

The crowd roared with laughter as Bang Bang moved to stage left, the spotlight following her. A projector screen came into the blowing circle cast by the spotlight, and then the spotlight slowly started to dim. A picture was suddenly cast on the screen that was just above Bang Bang's head.

"I'm here to pay tribute to two of the ugliest queens this town has ever seen," She said. "And I mean that with all of the love in my heart."

The crowd "awwwwed" at her.

"For forty years, Vic and Harry Thomas have run this bar—*A Straight Line*—and it has been a beacon of hope for all of us. A safe space. A home. A place for our community to come together. A place to get chlamydia or a good hamburger."

Laughter rolled through the crowd.

"It has been my home away from home for four decades," Bang Bang said as she pointed up at the screen, which I suddenly realized was a picture of my uncles, "all because these two men up there had a vision for Littleburg. *A Straight Line.* The best little queer bar in all of the Midwest. You know how this bar got its name?"

Everyone responded with a round of "no's" once more.

"Well, we thought having 'straight' in the name would confuse the cops first of all," Bang Bang chuckled. "Of course, on the first night we were open, we had to assure the queers that the straight line we were talking about was the line to the gloryholes!"

Everyone was laughing uproariously yet again. Then Bang Bang drew everyone's attention back to the picture over her head on the projection screen. The crowd made appreciative noises again as Bang Bang looked up at the picture lovingly.

"I took that picture of them while we were all in Greece years and years ago," She sighed. "A bunch of queers in Greece. Just like Broadway."

More laughter.

"Look at those two." She shook her head. "Never a bit of fashion sense. Even with me as a friend, they never could figure out how to dress. Those shirts. The pants. Those shoes! Whoever would have thought those leathery, worn-out things were cute? The shoes are pretty bad, too!"

We all erupted with laughter again, and I could see that Harry and Vic were enjoying the roasting as much as the rest of us.

"Speaking of leathery, worn-out things, has anyone seen Felix's testicles?" She asked.

The crowd laughed uproariously, and I smiled when Denny laughed harder than anyone.

"Felix?" Bang Bang brought a hand over her eyes again to peer out into the crowd. "Where are you, you worn-out old trick?"

A sharp whistle came from the area by the bar, and we all turned our heads to find Felix waving his middle finger in the air at Bang Bang on the stage.

"Oh, calm down," Bang Bang said. "I was just wondering if you'd thought about a trip to Michael's is all!"

Laughter pealed through the bar once again as Bang Bang continued her show. For the next several minutes, Bang Bang showed more pictures she had of the elder gays, telling stories of the bar's history, what part each of the men played in its opening—and staying open. Thankfully, she also included the other drag queens, Bethany, other lesbians, our trans family, and others. Of course, each story was punctuated with a crude joke at each one's expense. The drag queens who had been tending bar began moving about the room, delivering more beers and shots, and the crowd got drunker and rowdier, interacting more and more with Bang Bang as she carried on about *A Straight Line* and all of the queers in the community who had meant something in the span of its history.

Finally, after roasting everyone thoroughly, Bang Bang treated us all to her lip-sync version of *I Will Survive* by Gloria Gaynor. Maybe it was a little trite, but considering how she had just finished her roast with talking about how the bar would be a lasting landmark in the community, even if Harry and Vic had decided it was time to move on, it was fitting. Finally, the rest of the drag queens joined Bang Bang on stage and performed a rousing lip-sync to *I'm Coming Out* by Diana Ross. As the queens did their lip-sync, several party attendees got on the dance floor and kicked up their heels.

When all was said and done, and the queens were exiting the stage, leaving Bang Bang to wave and say "thank you," the crowd couldn't be tamed. Hoots and hollers, snaps, and whistles echoed through the bar as Bang Bang waved over and over again, blowing kiss after kiss in the direction of Harry's and Vic's table. Even when Bang Bang exited the stage, through the curtains at the back, instead of down the stairs at the front like the rest of the queens, the crowd remained rowdy. It wasn't until the other queens were behind the bar and serving drinks again, and more music was being played that everyone started to focus elsewhere.

For all the laughing I had done and the joy I had felt for the half-hour Bang Bang was on stage, I suddenly felt sullen again. Seeing Bang Bang on stage, fearlessly working the crowd, making everyone laugh, had filled me with a joy I hadn't felt in a long time. Now that it was all over, and I knew the party was going to come to an end eventually, all I felt was empty. And maybe a little drunk from the shots and beers we'd had since we got to the bar. When I felt Denny nudge me in the side, I looked over to find him gazing at me imploringly. His eyes darted between me and the dance floor.

I wanted to scream.

"Hey," I said, distracting him, "I just want to go say 'hi' to Bang Bang before she disappears for God knows how long."

I had to shout to be heard over the music and the crowd.

"When you're done, we'll dance?" Denny asked, hopefully.

"I mean, yeah. We'll see. Okay?" I shouted back.

"Yeah," Denny said. "All right."

He didn't say anything else. Instead, he turned on his heels and walked away. I watched him as he made his way through the crowd and over to Harry's and Vic's table, where a group of people was waiting to say a nice word or two to the soon-to-be-former owners of *A Straight Line*. The way his shoulders were hunched, and how he shuffled his feet, I could tell Denny was upset.

Why am I such a dick?

Chapter 12
Because That's Just What We Do

"Come in!" Bang Bang's muffled response reached my ears through the dressing room door at the back of the club.

I had just knocked on the door and had leaned closer to listen for a response. The music and the sound of the partygoers were nearly deafening, so I didn't want to miss being told to "enter" if Bang Bang actually heard the knock over everything else. As soon as I heard her response, I pushed the door open a crack, hesitant at first at intruding on her downtime after the show she had just given for free in honor of Harry and Vic. However, history told me that nothing set me right like a chat with Bang Bang, no matter how brief. Everything in the day had been leading up to getting a moment to at least say a few words to her, and having a few words returned.

Maybe it's not widely known outside of the LGBTQ-plus community, but those in the community know it to be true—a drag queen is always the best person to go to when you need advice. Or a laugh. Or just to commiserate. They are the wisest and kindest of all queers—even if they sometimes make a living reading other people to filth. I had never been what most people would call "close" with Bang Bang, but she had always been a permanent fixture in my life. Being my uncles' best friend meant that she was always nearby at all times, hovering over us like some tarted out, busted, fairy godmother.

I took a deep breath and pushed the door the rest of the way open, swinging it wide until I saw Bang Bang sitting at her dressing and makeup table across the room. Our eyes caught each other in the mirror over the table, and she looked confused for a moment. Then, recognition shot through her eyes, and her mouth turned up in a pleased smile. This, of course, brought a smile to my face as well. We hadn't seen each other since before I was in college, but she recognized me. That alone, recognition from Bang Bang, was enough to bring back the joy I had lost minutes before. For a few moments, we just stared at each other in the mirror, then Bang Bang shook her head.

"Close the door!" She ordered. "Half the fucking bar will be in here in seconds if they think there's another place to get their dicks out, Russy!"

I laughed as I quickly stepped inside the room and shut the door behind me gently, then put my back against it.

"Well, look at you," She said, still gazing at me through the mirror. "I haven't seen you in…five, six years?"

"Something like that. Maybe longer." I shrugged, suddenly feeling guilty at my desire to see Bang Bang so desperately, yet having not visited in so long.

"And why is that?" She turned on her stool and jabbed her hands into her hips. "Are we not good enough for you down here in bum-fuck-Ioway or what?"

I couldn't help but laugh again. Another shrug.

"Life?" I suggested. "Life always gets in the way of visits, right?"

"I know Harry and Vic didn't take that as an excuse over the years," Bang Bang said, "so it's not going to work with me either."

"I kind of thought maybe you would have forgotten me by now," I said.

Bang Bang's face softened.

"What a thing to say!" She exclaimed, rising from her stool to reach out to me.

Each finger was adorned with a long nail painted expertly in a flaming candy red. Blindingly brilliant jewels were set in rings on nearly every finger. Obviously, the jewelry was fake. Bang Bang wasn't that famous of a drag queen. The red sequined floor-length gown, fitted perfectly to Bang Bang's body, with sleeves that ran down to mid-forearm, twinkled in the lights. Her cotton-candy white wig, styled in a giant, almost-bouffant, was still atop her head, and not a lick of makeup was out of place. A large feathery flower was jammed into the wig at the side. Her high heels were the only component she had removed since entering the dressing room. When I thought about wearing high heels for any length of time, my legs hurt, so I could imagine that taking them off after any performance, no matter how short that performance had been, was probably orgasmic. A quick glance around the room and I spotted the patent leather heels tucked neatly away under the dressing table.

"How could I forget you?" Bang Bang asked as I stepped forward to take her hands in mine. "How many of my best friends of mine do you think have a nephew who is my favorite?"

"Liar." I was only half teasing.

"You ask Harry and Vic," Bang Bang said, pulling me in for a cheek kiss, "I ask about you every time that we get together."

"I believe you," I said, kissing her cheek.

Bang Bang popped me under the chin playfully as we pulled out of our embrace. She gestured for me to take a seat in a chair that was at the side of her dressing table, then she elegantly returned to her stool, gazing at herself in the mirror over the table. For a few moments, I watched her as she touched up her lipstick and eyeliner and adjusted her wig, though none of it was out of place. Once she was done with her wig and makeup, she adjusted the fake boobs that were stuffed down the front of her gown, and then turned on her stool to look at me again.

"So?" She asked.

"I just thought I'd come say 'hi' since I haven't seen you in forever," I said.

"Well, I don't know much about being a rancher, but I know bullshit when I smell it," She said. "You don't look like you just wanted to say 'hi' to me."

She said the last part in a mocking tone, though a smile formed on her face to take the sting out of her impression of me.

"Well, I mean, yeah, I wanted to say 'hi' to you and all."

"And?" She asked.

"And to thank you for doing such a wonderful thing for Harry and Vic," I said. "For a while, I thought you weren't going to show. I'm sorry for thinking that—I mean, I should have known you would. You're their oldest and dearest friend. But, well, it really made this night extra special for them. Especially since you hired those fake cops to bring everyone over here and do your farewell performance for them in their bar. Even if it won't be their bar much longer."

"Those weren't *fake cops*." Bang Bang waved me off. "Those are the new owners of the bar. I'm surprised Harry and

Vic didn't recognize them immediately. It was probably the uniforms."

"What?" I laughed.

"Oh, yes," She said. "I told them that it would do them good to be seen helping out celebrating the end of an era with Harry and Vic. They're taking over a dynasty, honey. There has to be a proper changing of the guards, after all. This bar means something to this community—both to queers and non-queers. It represents this damn city moving out of the dark ages and into enlightenment. The dawning of a new era. Also, ripping their shirts open was my idea. If the boys know the new owners have pecs, well, that'll keep 'em coming back for more, right?"

Bang Bang winked at me, and I was laughing more.

"Nothing like a good deed and firm pecs to get the queers coming out in droves, right?" She quipped.

"I suppose so." I agreed.

"So," She said, "what's really got you in here looking like someone who hasn't got a friend in the world, Russy?"

Bang Bang turned to the mirror and started looking herself over again, giving me a moment to gather my thoughts.

"I guess," I began, "I guess I just needed to be around someone who exudes joy, I guess?"

"*I guess, I guess, I guess.*" She shook her head. "Do you know how old I am, Russy? I don't have time for you to beat around the bush. Landing strips are the rage right now anyway, so land the plane. Now, tell me what has you looking so glum. I've known you since you barely came up to my knee, and I know when something is wrong."

"In all fairness," I said, "with the heels you wear, it would take anyone a while to grow tall enough to go past your knee."

Bang Bang cackled. I hadn't been lying. Without heels, she was easily six-foot-three. With the heels…well, she was practically a giant.

"That's fair," She said. "But out with it. Eventually, your uncles are going to expect me to come out there and pretend I give a shit about their retirement, even though they're selling the bar we've all come to think of as a second home over the years!"

"Actually," I asked, "what are you going to do? Are you retiring from the biz?"

Bang Bang smiled.

"The pecs aren't the only nice thing about the new owners," She said. "They've guaranteed me twice weekly shows. Until I can't get on the stage without a walker. Even then, I guess they'll just wheel me out onto the dance floor to tell my dick jokes."

I smiled. "So, you'll still be around if I need a smile?"

Bang Bang leaned in. "I'm here now. That's more important."

I just stared at her.

"I see that look in your eyes," She sighed. "What's his name? Is it that boy you were shacked up with after college?"

"What?" I chuckled nervously.

"I told you I always asked Vic and Harry about you." She shook a finger at me. "I've had my nose all in your business without you knowing."

"Yeah," I said, "I mean, yeah. Him. Clint."

"Clint." Bang Bang looked thoughtful. "What a shit name."

I laughed. "Well, he's kind of a shit person."

"Cheat on you, did he?"

"No," I said, "nothing like that."

"Give you crabs?"

"No!"

"Steal your wallet and your favorite casserole dish?"

"What?"

"Sorry. PTSD." She waved me off. "So? What did *Clint* do?"

I sighed. "He decided he didn't love me as much as I loved him."

"Mmmm." Bang Bang pursed her lips. "He use those exact words?"

I shrugged. "Yeah."

"How long did it take him to figure that out?"

"Three years." I groaned.

"Bastard." Bang Bang shook her head.

"I know, right?"

"I hope you tossed his ass to the curb, Russy."

"No," I said, "I was stupid and tried to make him want to stay. I'm a fucking idiot."

"Hey, now," She said as she turned away from the mirror to grab my hand, "you're not an idiot for trying to hold onto something you loved. Maybe a pushover, but not an idiot."

"Maybe," I laughed, "but I can't shake it, Bang Bang. I always grew up thinking that husbands loved wives. And husbands loved husbands. You get the idea."

She nodded.

"Harry and Vic have always been deeply in love," I continued, "and my dad always loved my mom. Why didn't Clint love me? I think I loved him enough."

Bang Bang stared deeply into my eyes.

"Why was I not good enough?" I asked no one. "I mean, if some guy who stayed with me for three years for—for—whatever reason—couldn't make himself *love me enough*, then maybe I'm just not lovable? Maybe every guy will decide

I'm not worth loving after they've gotten to know me better and wasted years of my life, ya' know?"

"It's not you. It's him." Bang Bang squeezed my hand. "You know what? Maybe Clint didn't mean to hurt you. He's a bastard, but his intentions might have been in the right place. Maybe he thought it would work, and he didn't want to hurt you by sharing any doubts he had before the moment it all went to hell? He might have meant well, but in the end, he still ended up hurting you. We'll never know the truth because there's no point in finding him and asking. But I will tell you one thing—you can't start feeling better until you realize that one sorry ass man with *possibly* good intentions isn't the end of the world. Strike one. Get back up to bat. The next one might be a home run."

"What if I end up striking out?"

"Well, what the fuck else you gotta do? Sit on the bench and watch everyone else play? If there's one thing I know about baseball—it's a lot more fun to play than it is to watch. And I've played it in full drag for charity before."

I laughed. "I wish I'd seen that."

"It was before you were even born," She said. "And I'm too old now to be running around in heels. Unless I'm getting paid."

"So," I shrugged, "what do I do?"

Bang Bang turned on the stool to look at me, and both of my hands were suddenly in hers as she looked deeply into my eyes.

"You know," She said, "I never expected to ever be loved. My parents didn't love me. A boy who liked wigs, makeup, dresses, and show tunes? Forget about it. They'd have rather been shot in the head than accept me. My friends all rejected me. When I met your uncles, I didn't have a friend in the world left to call my own. We were all in our thirties then. I had been alone for so long. Sometimes, when you least expect it, you find what you need, Russy."

"Can you call me 'Russ'?" I found myself asking suddenly.

"Of course," She said.

"I don't really like 'Russy,'" I said.

"You might want to tell a few people."

I rolled my eyes with a chuckle. "I know, right?"

"Stop being a doormat and stand up for yourself, Russ," She said. "And when an opportunity walks into your life, don't be a big ole sourpuss and ignore it. Before you know it, there'll be another guy begging for your attention. And he'll love you back enough. More than enough."

I just stared at her.

"You believe me, don't you?"

"Sure," I said. "I mean, Harry has Vic. Mom has Dad. The Flirtatious Five have all had each other at one point or another."

Bang Bang cackled. "Those old queens! I couldn't even be bothered to keep up with who was sliding into whose bed most of the time way back when."

"Right?"

Bang Bang reached up and brushed a thumb over my cheek.

"Why don't you get out there and find a hot young guy to dance with?" She suggested. "Have a drink. Get your confidence back? You'll be right as rain before you know it."

"Yeah, maybe," I said. "Hey, Vic said I'd get to meet Robert tonight?"

Bang Bang looked pained.

"Your...uh, your husband? Boyfriend? Partner?" I asked. "He didn't really say if you guys were married or whatever, but—"

Bang Bang began reaching into her cleavage, making me stop short of whatever brilliant thing I was trying to think of to say but was failing at miserably. Cautiously, I watched as she dug around in her fake boobs, looking for something only she knew about. Finally, after a little digging, she pulled a charm out of her dress that was attached to a necklace I hadn't noticed before. The necklace was silver, dulled by age, and the charm at the end simply looked like a little vial but was made of silver just like the chain.

"What's that?" I asked.

"Robert," She said. "The rest of him is in an urn over the fireplace at home."

"That's…?"

"Ashes, yes," She said. "Well, a teensy, tiny little bit. That's so he can be with me wherever I go. Trying to get cremains through airport security is always a hassle, so…I keep a bit of him here by my heart. The rest has to stay at home and wait for me to return. He was always a homebody after he gave up being a traveling salesman anyway, so I think this is what he'd have preferred."

For the longest of moments, Bang Bang held the charm out to me, and I just stared at it, suddenly realizing what Vic had meant when he said that *if Bang Bang is coming, so is Robert.*

"When did he…?"

"Oh, my goodness," Bang Bang slid the charm back inside her dress to rest between the fake boobs, "ten years now it's been. He was older than me, you know. I'm surprised I had him as long as I did. I wish I'd thought to have you meet him when the chance was there."

"You met him the night before the bar opened?"

"Yes." She was delighted that I knew that. "Just wandered in off the street like a puppy. He was much to preppy for my tastes. I usually like 'em a bit rough—if you know what I mean."

I chuckled nervously.

"But he came in looking for a bathroom in a three-piece suit, leather dress shoes—he looked like he was ready to try and sell encyclopedias or a burial plot to us." Bang Bang slapped at my knee. "I certainly didn't think he was sniffing around for some tail, either. But who woulda thunk it—a few months later, we were living together and happy as could be. And I found out he could be a little rough around the edges like I enjoyed."

She winked at me, which made my cheeks warm as I chuckled at her comment.

"You know," She said, patting the place on her chest where the charm was buried in her dress, "I considered telling him to get lost that night—when it became apparent he was trying to be *friendly* with me, I mean. Once he realized what kind of bar he had wandered into, he figured out what kind of men he was amongst, and he set about getting cozy with me. I didn't want none of it. But something deep inside of me said: *'Morty, you slept with half of New York for a place to sleep before. You can sleep with a guy in a three-piece suit because you're bored.'* Well, I'm glad I listened to that voice because I wasn't bored another night of my life until he was gone."

"What did he...die from? If that's not too personal?"

"Oh, the cancer, you know?" Bang Bang sighed. "Once you get to mine and your uncles' age—the age Robert was then—you either die in your sleep, or you get cancer. Or a heart attack. You're really on borrowed time. I'm just glad I can strut around in heels without throwing out a hip, honestly."

"That's so sad."

"Is it?" Bang Bang looked at me. "We had thirty good years together. You can't really be mad at death if it waits long enough to let you enjoy yourself with the love of your life first."

"I guess?"

"I know so," Bang Bang said. "But if you go through life with your thumb up your ass, afraid to get your heart broken, ignoring that voice that tells you to take the leap, the thirty years you might've had turns into twenty. Then ten. Then nine, eight...then nothing. You'll just end up a dusty old queen wishing you hadn't been so bitter."

"I got it, I got it," I laughed.

"Good." She slapped my knee and turned back to the mirror as I rose from the chair. "Now that I've sorted you out, get out there and have that dance and drink. I'll be out shortly to talk to your uncles. Save a dance for me, would you?"

"Uh, yeah. I don't dance."

"What?" Bang Bang looked scandalized. "You don't dance?"

"I'm a bad dancer." I shrugged.

"Russ," She said, "the best thing about dancing is that you don't have to be any good at it to enjoy it. You do it simply because it's fun."

"I suppose…"

"Especially if you have somebody cute to do it with."

"Are you talking about yourself or some guy in the bar?" I teased.

"Obviously, I'm talking about myself," Bang Bang said, "but if I get out there and find you grabbed some other cute guy, I won't hold it against you."

With a laugh, I headed to the door as Bang Bang began picking at her wig in the mirror. Obviously, she needed to look perfect before she went out to the bar once again. When I reached the door, I craned my neck to look at Bang Bang once again.

"Hey," I said, "thanks again."

"What for, Russ?"

"This." I gestured vaguely. "For Harry and Vic. For the community. For listening."

"Oh," She sighed, "no need to thank me. That's just what we do."

"Drag queens?"

"No," She said, "the community. When we need each other, we show up. When one of us shines, we all shine."

I smiled. "I'll try to remember that."

"Good." She winked.

"Hey," I said, "if you...*or Morty*...ever need me to show up, I'll be there. Bang Bang is awesome, but I've heard some pretty great things about Morty, too."

Bang Bang smiled. "That's just about the nicest thing anyone's ever said to me, Russ."

I almost turned to the door again but stopped myself.

"Hey."

"Yes?" She asked, looking unbothered, but I knew I had to be on her last nerve.

"Your wallet and...*a casserole dish?*"

"Girl, did you know it was Le Creuset!?" She screamed as she spun on the stool to face me. "And that was back when I didn't have the money to just go out and buy a new casserole dish! You can't trust any ole trick! I'm *still* pissed, and I *have* money now!"

I laughed loudly. *Le Creuset.* She didn't even care about the wallet.

Bang Bang gave me another wink, then turned back to the mirror. So, I stepped out of the back room and shut the door gently behind myself. The sound of thumping dance music and the crowd of people in the bar reached my ears, turning my body into a live wire once more. However, after talking to Bang Bang, I felt lighter. The noise wasn't quite as overwhelming as it could have been. I walked down the hallway and made my way back out into the bar, hoping Bang Bang would show up soon to talk to Harry and Vic. It would be an even more perfect ending to the night for them.

Out in the main room of the bar, the crowd had thinned around my uncles, and they were sitting at their table, their hands held on the top it, two beers in front of them, as they watched everyone dancing to a Britney Spears song with glee. I stood there for a moment on the periphery of the party, a smile coming to my face at seeing the absolute, unfiltered joy on their faces. Almost fifty years of partnership, forty years of owning *A Straight Line*, and they looked as happy and as in love as I'd ever seen them.

Maybe it's not all pointless? I thought to myself.

I wound my way through the crowd over to their table, and when they saw me, both of their eyes lit up. Both of them rose to greet me, wrapping their arms around me in turn. I couldn't really hear much of what they said over the music and the crowd, but I was pretty sure they were telling me how grateful and happy they were. The evening had been everything they had hoped for and more. They had their bar, their best friends, their community, everything they'd ever loved around them for one perfect ending to cap off a perfect era of their lives together. When we're all older, and in the twilight years of our lives, what more could anyone possibly wish for, really?

Looking out over the crowd of queer people dancing on the floor to contemporary pop hits, their arms flailing about, smiles slashed across their faces as they danced with friends, lovers, strangers—or any combination thereof, I couldn't help but smile. All genders, races, orientations, shapes and sizes, had come together to pay tribute to forty years of having a safe space to call our own. Even though the world was getting better, *A Straight Line* would never not be our home away from home. Because no matter how much better the world got, the bar had been there for all queers when the rest of the world wasn't. That was worth honoring every night that we had the chance.

As I looked out at the sea of different faces on the dance floor, I couldn't help but realize that I didn't know most of them. Most of them didn't know me. Hopefully, that would change in the future. But in the meantime, I didn't know any of their stories. And none of them knew mine. There were plenty of stories, just like mine, but special in their own way. Dancing in front of me were people in love, people whose hearts had been broken, people who had been rejected by their families. There were people who had experienced racism, homophobia, misogyny, violence…but also love and friendship and…*life*. Maybe the good had outweighed the bad in their stories. And perhaps the bad overwhelmed the good.

But either way, they chose to dance.

Vic and Harry motioned for me to pull up a chair and share their table with them. And I almost did. Instead, I gestured that I would be back later. Then we could sit back and enjoy the spectacle before us together.

I didn't know where I'd find Denny, but I tried scanning the dance floor first. Maybe he had found Officer Michael so that he'd have a willing dance partner? I couldn't find him amongst the flailing bodies, so I checked the other tables in the seating area, hoping maybe he was with his grandfather. When I found Felix, he was holding court with the other elders in The Flirtatious Five, as well as Bethany and a few other of the "aged lesbians." They were all regaling each other with stories, which they had to scream to each other to be heard since they were so close to the dance floor. But Denny wasn't with them.

Back over at Harry's and Vic's table, I saw that Bang Bang had arrived, and she was pulling up a chair to sit with them, which warmed my heart and brought the smile back to my face. Finally, I forced myself to head over to the bar. It was the only part of the bar that was somewhat insulated from the music, so maybe Denny had gone there for a respite?

When I got to the bar, it was fairly packed with a bunch of partygoers, trying to get as sloshed as possible before the party ended. I just imagined the drag queens trying to get everybody on the buses at dawn so they could be delivered back to Harry's and Vic's. A lot of people would be borrowing floor space and spare beds and the couches to sleep off the booze before heading home later in the day. Harry and Vic would love it.

Denny was at the far end of the bar when I finally laid eyes on his back. No one seemed to be with him, and he was nursing a beer. He didn't look like he wasn't having fun, but he didn't look like he was having as much fun as he wanted, either. So, I made my way through the smaller crowd to the end of the bar where he was and tapped him on his shoulder. Denny turned around, beer still in hand, to see who was trying to get his attention.

"Hey," I said.

He gave me a half-smile. "Hey."

"Look," I said, swallowing my doubt, "I thought, maybe, you know, if you still wanted to give me your number. Maybe, you know…sometime…if you wanted…yeah. Tonight doesn't have to be the only night we, uh, hang out. If you still want that and all?"

Denny stared at me for a moment, leaving me in suspense, but finally, his smile grew.

"Yeah," He said. "I still want that and all."

"Great." I dug my phone out of my pocket, unlocked it, and passed it to him.

Denny pushed buttons rapidly, then handed it back.

"Mission accomplished," He said.

Also," I said, sliding the phone back into my pocket, "I wanted to know if you used up all of your dances? Or are you still saving one for me?"

Denny's face broke into a grin.

"Yeah," He said. "I've saved one for you."

"I don't dance well at all," I warned him. "I'm a horrible dancer. Just so you know."

Denny slammed the rest of his beer and put the empty bottle on the bar, then turned back to me.

"Maybe we'll have to dance through a few songs, then?" He suggested. "Until you get the hang of it?"

"Fine." I rolled my eyes playfully.

With that, Denny grabbed my hand, lacing his fingers through mine, and pulled me towards the dance floor. *Born This Way* by Lady Gaga began pouring out of the speakers as we reached the edge of the dance floor, causing every queer in the room to go wild.

"Hey," I stopped Denny to scream over the music, suddenly self-conscious again, "don't judge me."

Denny smiled at me and gripped my hand tighter.

"That's something we do *not* do here," He leaned in to shout in my ear.

With a wary smile, I let Denny lead me through the throngs of flailing arms and undulating bodies to the very center of the dance floor. We got right in the middle where everyone could see us, and I did my best. My arms probably flailed around the wrong way. I'm pretty sure I was stepping on Denny's toes. Sweat started to form on my forehead almost immediately due to being surrounded by so many warm bodies in such a small space. It definitely wasn't cute. I probably looked like I was having a fit of some kind, right there in the center of what would soon no longer be my uncles' bar. But we celebrated our community and its history. We danced.

Because that's just what we do.

The End.

About the Authors

J.D. Wade is a retired man, enjoying post-career life in the Pacific Northwest of the United States with his life-long partner, now husband. In his spare time, he enjoys writing, woodworking, long hikes in the woods, playing with his two dogs, and trying new foods and drinks. He can be reached through www.thelionfishpress.com or thelionfishpress@thelionfishpress.com.

Chase Connor currently lives in Des Moines, Iowa with his husband, his dog, Rimbaud, and spends his days writing about the people who live (loudly and rent-free) in his head when he's not busy being enthusiastic about naps and Pad Thai. Chase started his writing career as a confused gay teen looking for an escape from reality. Ten years later, one of the books he wrote during those years, *Just A Dumb Surfer Dude: A Gay Coming-of-Age Tale*, was published independently. Now with The Lion Fish Press (and almost 20 books later), Chase has numerous projects in various stages of completion and lined up for publishing. Chase is a multi-genre author, but always with a healthy dollop of gay.
Chase can be reached at
chaseconnor@chaseconnor.com
Or on Twitter @ChaseConnor7
Or on Facebook https://www.facebook.com/Chase-Connor-Books-101655541691343
He can also be found on Chase Connor Books
https://chaseconnor.com
or on Goodreads
https://www.goodreads.com/author/show/18055910.Chase_Connor
He does his very best to respond to all DMs, emails, and Twitter comments from his reader friends and loves the interaction with them. Chase has several novellas/novels for sale on Amazon (and other sites) in ebook and paperback format.

Chase Connor's catalog can be read for free with Kindle Unlimited

www.ingramcontent.com/pod-product-compliance
Lightning Source LLC
Chambersburg PA
CBHW070919180626
46817CB00003B/1132